Binding of the Almatraek

Book Four:

Foresight's Flight

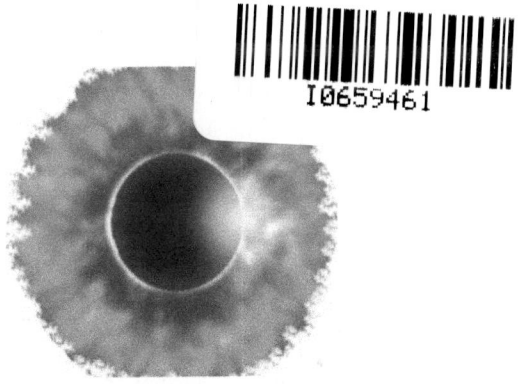

Heather Reilly

Published by Reilly Books
at Createspace
www.reillybooks.com

ISBN: 978-0-9950999-2-0

Acknowledgments

Research plays a big role when writing about a specific time period. This usually entails countless hours (often more than what is put into the actual writing), in order to make sure that the story is told properly. It simply wouldn't do to mention an electric refrigerator in the middle ages, or to make references to other things that weren't invented yet. But sometimes, simply reading articles, books, and websites can't answer the questions you have about a certain topic. This is when I turn to people who are experts in their field.

Therefore, I would very much like to take the opportunity to thank Master Falconer Lydia Ash, who was able to give me insight into how a falcon might behave in certain situations. She was kind enough to let me pick her brain about one of Oslan's favourite pass-times, and her website, The Modern Apprentice, offers a wealth of information on the sport of Falconry. Please support her and visit her website at:

http://www.themodernapprentice.com

Other Books by the Author

Novels:
Binding of the Almatraek Series
Book 1: Knight's Surrender
Book 2: Noble Pursuit
Book 3: Enchanted Page

2 Stories in Engen's *Fantasy on the Rock:*
"In the Moonlight"
"Test of the Sihn Du"

Children's Storybooks:
The Tree and the Sun
Tock Tick Tock, the Mouse and the Clock
The Poetical Alphabetical Book

Illustrations:
Santa Almost Missed our Town
An Old Time Christmas
Santa Really Does Know

Games:
Cauldron Cards
Cauldron Cards Expansion Pack
Kingdom

Upcoming books:
Melody's Marvelous Mixture

To learn more about the author or her books, visit

www.booksofafeather.weebly.com
or
www.reillybooks.com

Dedication

This book is dedicated, to my wonderfully enthusiastic students at Whitbourne Elementary School. Keep your dreams alive, I believe in you.

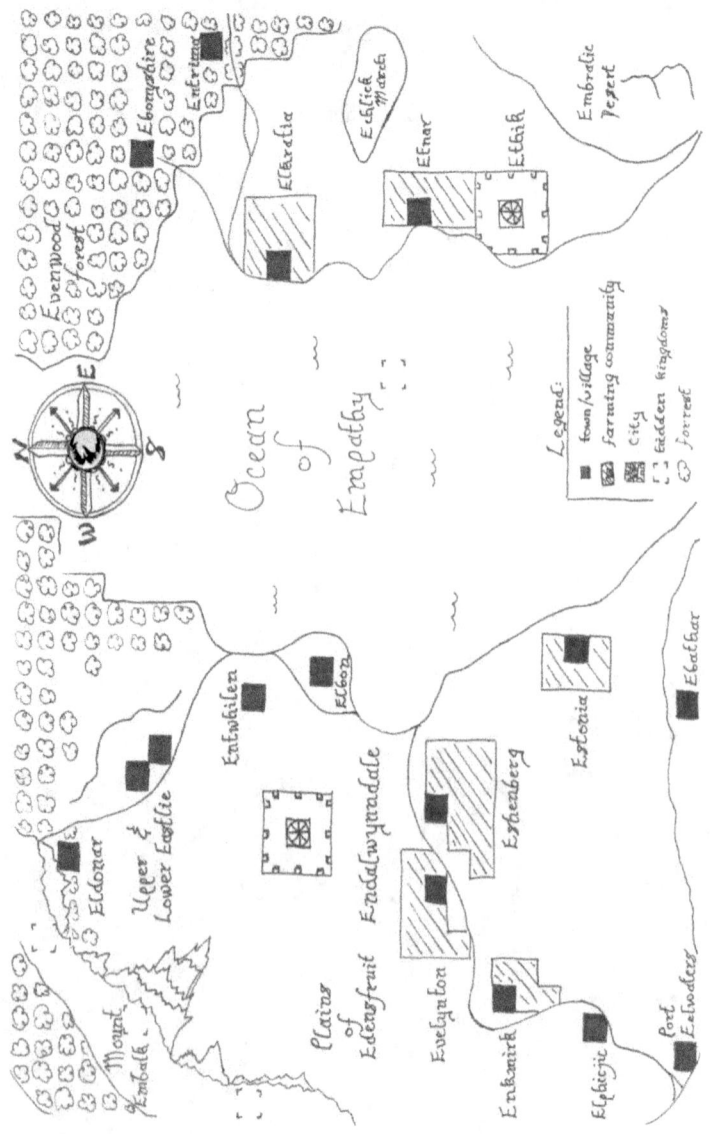

Chapter 1
O Blinded by the Dark O

Sasha's eyes flew open in the dark as her panic stricken breath caught in her throat. The room was so seamlessly black that at first she wasn't sure as to whether or not she was still dreaming. Then, one of the miniscule beads of perspiration that dotted her forehead trickled down to her temple, and she was able to swallow back the scream that had been threatening to pierce the night.

She sat up in her large canopied bed, shakily pulling her knees to her chest and hugging the covers to her chin for comfort. Her nightgown clung to her back in a cold sweat, and she could feel that her normally luxurious long waterfall of golden hair was currently a plastered down mess of tangles.

"Sabyn?" Sasha quietly croaked into the night with a voice that seemed reluctant to work. She wanted a candle and some company to sooth her frayed nerves. She was rewarded by the muffled sigh of someone in a deep sleep. Apparently her handmaid would be of little help right now. Determined to have some light, Sasha dangled her long legs over the side of her feather mattress and felt for the cold flagstones with her toes. She shuffled to the table and fumbled for something to light the candlestick with. As her delicate fingers fanned out blindly across the cool wooden surface, her wrist caught the base of the candlestick holder, and sent the whole works toppling over the edge.

The meaty thud that followed was accompanied by an incensed "Ouch!"

"Oh, Sabyn, I'm terribly sorry." Sasha confessed with a somewhat stronger voice. She was pretty sure that the relief she felt at the girl's waking had been masked by the sincerity of her apology, after all, she was sorry that the girl had had a candle stick dropped on her head, even if she was also glad that she was no longer alone in the dark.

Sasha heard the clunk of the metal being replaced on the table, and after a few short seconds of letting Sabyn handle things, a glorious little spark sprang to life, lighting the candle and casting a soft glow about the room. The green eyes of her maid seemed to be taking her shaken appearance in, and the girl instantly jumped to work, making Sasha feel more secure by the minute. Sabyn's tight brown curls bounced as she bounded across the room to fetch her mistress a clean nightgown, and swapped it out for the sweat-stained one the taller girl had been wearing. Then, leading Sasha by the hand, Sabyn delivered her to the seat in front of the table where her comb, silver handled brush, and mirror waited. First the girl took up a section of Sasha's hair and deftly worked out some of the knots with the comb and finger tips. Then she began the arduous task of brushing each section one hundred times with long sure strokes until they once again shone. With the familiar sensation of each pass of the brush, Sasha became increasingly more relaxed.

"Would you have me call for a bath?" the girl offered.

"Not a bath, that will take too long. I think that I would rather have some tea." Sasha confided.

"Right away, Milady." Sabyn acknowledged, and quickly quitted the room.

Sasha had never been afraid of the gloom of the night, even on cloudy starless evenings that afforded no light from the heavens above. But, for the last few weeks, sheer darkness had become more and more frequent, like a great eclipse rolling across the face of her visions.

At eighteen, Sasha's talents had been kept secret from the kingdom for well over a decade. No one suspected that the lady that had often been seen in the company of Queen Aylan, was what the king considered to be his secret weapon. With her willowy height, fine dresses of gold, and sure and proper manner, no one questioned her upbringing. The truth was though, that she was a regular peasant who had lived in the castle as a noble for almost her whole life.

Since she had been a toddler, Sasha's dreams had been able to foretell future events. When one of her dreams had ended up saving an entire village from burning, the town guard there had brought word to the castle. The king had been no fool. Their kingdom had enjoyed generations of peace, and having a reliable seer would perhaps help him to avoid war or attacks from other nations. Sasha's parents had loved their daughter greatly, and had wanted for her a better life than they could have given her. So when King Eurilas had offered to take her in to have her raised like one of his own, they had quickly agreed. But of course, she had been young and remembered very little of this. Castle life was the only life she knew.

Sasha's visions often came to her during her regular hours of sleep, although over the years, she had honed the ability to put herself into a trance in order to use her unusual gift almost at will. However, the visions that she normally had as Endalwynndale's seer only came to her in snippets as of late, which was very frustrating. Tonight for the first time though, she had been unable to see anything at all. It was terrifying. What if she was losing her gift? Without her ability that made her who she was, she would have no place here. In fact, it was so much a part of her that she was beginning to feel like she was losing her identity. She was falling apart.

A soft knocking at the door was accompanied by a hushed familiar voice.

"Sasha?" the whisper asked, "are you awake?" *Aylan,* she thought, relieved.

Sasha rushed across the room to open the door, ecstatic that her friend was here. Aylan's rounded belly came through the doorway as she waddled her way into the room. Slowly swaying, somehow gracefully, it wasn't lost on Sasha that the queen's pregnancy had made her as big as a house. Not that she would ever say anything, she knew how touchy the normally petit girl was about her temporary girth, and besides, it was never wise to anger a mage.

Sasha closed the door as Aylan made her way to one of the plush high-backed arm chairs that stood near the seer's fireplace. Bracing her hands on the wide arms of the chair, the queen awkwardly lowered herself down into the comfortable seat and sighed happily now that the weight had been taken off her feet. Sasha lifted the one lit candle to the wicks of two others to create more light for them to talk by. She was just sitting down in the other chair when Sabyn entered with a heavy silver tray. Sasha was expecting the teapot and the small bowl of honey, but she was surprised to see two teacups, an empty dish, and the whole cooked chicken that accompanied them.

"I passed Sabyn in the hall on the way to the kitchen, and asked her to bring a few extra things. Then I made my way here and hoped that you hadn't gone back to bed," Sasha's dear friend explained her.

Upon seeing the queen, Sabyn curtsied deeply and smiled brightly as she set down the tray before them.

"Glad to see you two made it here safely, Your Majesty." She welcomed the royal and babe in her tummy. For her part, Aylan caught Sasha balking at the steaming chicken, and flushed.

"I've been having the most bizarre cravings lately." She explained as if she couldn't quite believe it herself. Without further ado, she ripped off a drumstick and set to it with such zeal that it would have put some of the uncouth knights-in-training to shame.

Sasha merely cleared her throat in a ladylike fashion, and carefully poured the tea. Her actions seemed all the more delicate next to Aylan's, who had finished with the leg, and was now on to her second chicken wing.

As she waited for the tea to cool, Sasha began to tell Aylan about how her dreams had become dimmer by the day.

"It is as if the candle that helps me see is beginning to peter out," Sasha confided in distress. "My visions, whether in dream form or not, seem to be obstructed by something. It is as if I am trying to watch a play, but some tall bloke is seated in front of me, blocking my view of most of the show." She was getting frustrated just talking about it.

She reached for her cup of tea and asked Aylan, who was now slowing down with each mouthful, how Oslan had been handling the pregnancy.

"Oh, you know Oslan. He hardly leaves me alone for a second. Until he left on his horse this morning, I've had to sneak off to my work room just to get a second to myself. Even that has its drawbacks though. Since it's in a secret location, I can't even get the kitchen girls to bring me a snack there." she grumbled.

Sasha smirked. "You should consider turning your hidden room into a pantry."

Aylan actually seemed to consider it for a moment before her hand flew to her belly and her pretty face winced. "The babe is quite active now. The wee thing has given me no end of trouble when I cast." she told Sasha as her face slowly relaxed. "I have been working on a shielding spell, and I keep finding myself in the middle of holding it, and then this little one will kick me and break my concentration."

"I thought that Oslan had taught you to hold your spells even while...distracted." Sasha finished tactfully. She remembered how the king had tested Aylan's concentration by kissing her when their feelings for each other had still been brand new.

"Yes," Aylan replied, a grin spreading across her face, "but I've never had to complete an enchantment while in pain, thank the brightness. It's just so surprising when I can't see the impacts coming."

"I know what you mean," Sasha agreed ruefully. "I'm terrified that I'm going to miss something important, some piece of information, like before." As she reminisced, one or two uncomfortable butterflies began to flap around in her stomach. No, it wasn't as pleasant as that, it was more like a couple of impatient bats trying to find their way out of a cave.

Years ago, before Sasha had gained some modicum of control over her ability, she had been able to warn Oslan of another mage's plan that could have hurt the queen. Although she had misinterpreted the larger picture that the vision had presented, that had all turned out well. But in the same year, she had failed to see an attack on Oslan's father that had resulted in the previous king's death. Although neither Oslan, nor Aylan, had ever begrudged her missing that potential vision, Sasha had secretly beaten herself up over it emotionally for a year. She would never be able to forgive herself if anything happened to one of her friends in the same way. That is why she had begun to put herself into trances every day if she had received no premonitions during her sleep. She was determined never to miss an important vision again.

Aylan must have seen Sasha's countenance turn serious, because she abruptly put down the chicken breast that she had been eating, and wiped the grease from her fingertips with her napkin before putting a reassuring hand on her friend's arm.

"Worry not, Sasha, we always find a way through the dimness and back into the light." The queen took a sip of her own tea and added, "At least, we have so far."

Chapter 2
O Being Chosen O

The three adventurers lifted their hands in a final farewell, and turned from the great pyramid as the opening in the wall began to slide shut. The great sand-coloured bricks fit into place and ground to a halt. Even when looking for a crack or niche that might signify a way in, the unbreachable wall now looked seamless.

Lazelan, the former mage of Endalwynndale, pulled a square piece of cloth from his satchel and tied it down over his orangy-red curls before the desert sun could cause him discomfort. As soon as the cloth was placed between him and the glowing orb of heat in the sky, he began to feel marginally cooler. His loose-fitting light garments also helped with the heat.

The man to his right, Harmonium Magster, had done similarly. In his case, it also helped the ageless man to avoid getting sunburnt on his shining dome, although nothing protected his shirtless torso. Harmonium was a sort of untraditional monk, who had dedicated his plentiful years to the study of magic, nature, and empty-handed combat. He had been a master before teaching Lazelan at the university, and no one really knew how old he was.

Wolfbane Willowswitch was a different sort of fellow completely. The gnomish fighter insisted on using his short stature to his advantage, and simply walked in the shadow that Lazelan created to protect his uncovered head from the sun. He refused to doff his leather armour despite the heat, which quickly left him sweaty, although never irritable.

The men began trudging over the dunes along the wall of the pyramid while mulling over how they were going to cross the ocean and most of the land of the kingdom on the other side in order to get to their next destination. They were trying to hunt down the Almatraek Bright, a book of counter spells and antidotes for the evil contained within the pages of the Almatraek Dim, which had been used against the subjects of Endalwynndale.

The princess that lived within the pyramid had pointed them in the direction of Mount Embalk, a giant snow-covered rocky range that housed the clans of the dwarves. Their race was chiefly made up of miners and jewelers, however, two brothers that were both mages also lived among them within the frigid stony walls. These dwarves had harbored the Almatraek Bright at one time, and may have it still.

The three turned the corner and the sky was instantly filled with a thunder that made it seem as though the heavens were being torn asunder.

"Oh good, you didn't die." One of the sphinxes remarked lazily as his companion's continued deep purring made Lazelan's molars vibrate in his skull.

"That was *cat*egorically the most disappointing celebration of my wellbeing that I have ever heard." Wolfbane piped-up.

Lazelan groaned inwardly. The gnome's use of puns in any situation that presented itself was almost unbearable. The worst part was that to his astonishment, his own traitorous mind had begun mentally applauding Wolfbane's efforts. Then to his relief, the booming purring suddenly stopped.

"Can I eat him now?" The female sphinx asked. In answer, the male just smiled a wan smile, and used his great paw to push Wolfbane closer to his comrade.

"Just a moment," Harmonium interjected as the female smiled and licked her lips. Both cats slowly turned their great heads to look at him expectantly. "I would like to propose a deal."

"I'd love to hear all about it, right after I'm done this little snack." the female said silkily.

"Why would we make an accord with you when eating you would be so much more satisfying?" the male questioned.

"You can't eat me! The folk in the pyramid told us that once we had solved your riddles, we were untouchable."

"That only applies on the way in. Besides, even that is more of a guideline than a rule, really," the female feline cooed.

"It's a curtesy at best," the male agreed.

"We are not bound to any sort of agreement." The female confirmed. "This just seemed like a good place to wait for food that was guaranteed to come to us."

"Saves time on the hunting." the male grinned, revealing his pointed fangs.

"Oh, *purr*-fect." Wolfbane huffed, throwing up his hands.

Wait, did that sphinx just smile? Lazelan could have sworn that he saw the tips of the male's pointy canines in what could only have been described as a grin, before he feigned a huge slow yawn. The mage moved reflexively to stand beside his insufferable friend.

The humongous female cat got up and stretched with her tail high in the air and front paws extended past the edge of the platform she had been laying on. Loose sand cascaded down off of her back as she unfurled a gigantic set of wings. As she dipped her rib cage low enough to almost brush her platform, her rounded toes separated and extended to reveal a set of razor sharp claws.

This news was a shock to Lazelan. For his entire twenty-two years upon the planet, he had always been one to adhere to the rules; they were how he understood the world. Things had to adhere to the laws of nature; and people, to the laws of man. The fact that there were no rules where he had understood them to be put him off kilter. He thought that he had been protected by the fact that they had solved the sphinxes' queries to get into the pyramid in the first place. Now, with nowhere to run to and no armour, he felt completely exposed. He eyed the sigil of the hippogriff on Wolfbane's green dyed leather breastplate, and doubted that even that would be able to do anything to stop a sphinx's claws or teeth.

As the female straightened and made to come down to the sand where the adventurers stood, Harmonium slowly began to move. The bare-chested monk positioned himself so that he stood halfway between the gnome and the great cat. The thundering purring once again emanated from deep within the female sphinx's throat as she simply stepped over Harmonium and raised a paw, claws extended, to squash or slash at the little gnome.

Lazelan thought quickly and quietly uttered "Falfakti," *Shield,* to cast a protective barrier around himself. It was invisible, save for a slight bluish glow that seemed to hover about three inches from everything he wore and carried. He planted a hand firmly on the gnome's shoulder, and poured more energy into the spell. With the boost of power, the shield automatically extended around Wolfbane too.

Under the sphinx, Harmonium was weaving his hands around in the air in a familiar series of motions, which ended with him bringing his wrists together as he pushed his hands upward and uttered a strong "Oatas!" *Water.*

This was a similar spell that the seemingly ageless monk often used to call upon the rain to water his peony garden at home. Any bits of water vapour hovering in the air or in ancient underground streams long forgotten under the sand, quickly gathered and erupted in an intense geyser of fluid from where Harmonium stood, directly up onto the belly of the giant cat.

The sphinx yowled in shock and jumped vertically an impressive eighty feet into the air, landing twenty feet away. She quickly sat and began to lick the wet spot indignantly in quick short strokes.

"You didn't think it was going to be that easy, did you?" Wolfbane asked the cats, even though he had been the only one not to spring into action.

"Actually, no." the male answered, "But we do love to play with our food." he finished with a slightly menacing tone to his smooth baritone voice.

"As I was saying," Harmonium began to voice his idea as if nothing had happened, "We have to cross the desert, ocean, and kingdom on the other bank, and you two could save us a lot of time by giving us a lift." Harmonium concluded.

The male cat sat bolt upright. "Surely you don't mean that you expect to *ride* us like a common horse, mule, or camel?" he hissed as though he were scandalized.

"I have a counter offer," the female shared, "We'll carry you in our mouths, or more accurately, in our stomachs."

"Oh, what a wonderful idea!" purred the male in agreement. "We can pretty much guarantee that you'll arrive there, but we can't promise that it will be in one piece." he smiled dangerously.

"Actually, given your love of riddles, I was going to suggest a wager," Harmonium informed them. "I will present you with a riddle of my own. If you are unable to come up with the correct answer by the time the sun sets, then you will agree to carry us *safely* to our destination."

"And if we answer easily?" The male inquired.

"Well then, you can eat the gnome." He answered matter-of-factly.

"What?" Wolfbane called out in shock.

"Have you heard your terrible jokes?" Harmonium responded coolly, "I think it's a fair *pun*ishment."

Wolfbane started to sputter. "But, you just- that was pretty good, actually." he finished weakly.

"Oh I don't know," the female feline said, "I think he's a bit of a linguistic genius." Wolfbane smiled up at her winningly, and she returned an almost maternal smile of pride. "I bet you'll taste even better than most."

Wolfbane gulped audibly. The cats exchanged a look that seemed to hold an entire conversation. Then the female began to purr once again as the male grinned and said "We have an accord."

"Wait, I'm not agreeing to this! Why, none of you even considered to ask my opinion about this whole idea, and I think it stinks!" Wolfbane spat.

"Don't you trust me?" asked Harmonium in a calm and reassuring tone.

"Of *course* I don't! You just offered me up as cat food! One thing is for sure though; I'm not waiting around to become easy prey for these two. I'm out of here. If you get the urge, you can eat the monk instead."

"Tempting, but no thank you," sniffed the male sphinx. Lazelan noticed that the end of his tail had begun flicking to show his irritation. "That one is sunburnt, and if I wanted my food crispy, I'd be friends with a dragon."

Wolfbane began to trudge off, climbing a tall dune that would lead him away from the pyramid. For every three steps up the hill that he took in haste, Lazelan was pretty sure that he slid back two. The gnome was floundering. The mage shook his head in pity. He couldn't just stand here and watch this.

"You're going the wrong way!" Lazelan called after him. "The ocean is that way!" he shouted while pointing westward. Wolfbane glanced back and turned his course to the new direction. This time, he walked up the dune diagonally, which made his improved progress easier to watch.

"I'll go with him, master," Lazelan told the monk.

"Yes, keep him safe." the older man agreed like a father sending his older son to watch out for one much younger. Lazelan constantly wondered how old his old master from the university actually was. His best guess was that he was in fact at least twice as old as the forty-something years that he appeared to be. If they were in luck, the sphinxes might not have counted on how wise the old monk actually was. The sage just might have a riddle up his sleeve that the sphinxes hadn't heard before. Either way, Lazelan did trust Harmonium. He began to follow after Wolfbane, wondering what trick the old man had up his sleeve.

The sphinxes didn't seem to be perturbed in the least that their quarry was leaving.

"You do realize that you two are setting off into the desert, and there is nowhere to hide." The male called after them. "We will be able to find you in less time than it takes a sandstorm to cover a camel."

"Perhaps," Lazelan called back over his shoulder, "but it won't be until sunset."

The giant female cat began licking the side of her paw as if she'd lost interest in the whole encounter. Harmonium took a moment to gather his thoughts, and began reciting his riddle.

> *"As gigantic as a sphinx,*
> *Or as little as a flea,*
> *Both adults and younglings*
> *Have tried to keep me.*
> *I haven't got a face,*
> *Nor a body to hold,*
> *But I can be new,*
> *Or very very old.*
> *The person who shares me*
> *Will have given me away,*
> *And they can't take me back,*
> *I'll no longer stay."*

By the time he was done, both of the sphinxes had begun to give him their undivided attention.

"Oh, that's easy," the male answered almost immediately. "I now find myself quite disappointed, I really expected more from you. The answer of course, is *hope.*" he finished smugly.

"Come on now," the female chided her partner, "No it isn't. One doesn't lose hope once they've shared it with someone else. I've hoped for a long time that the princess would convince her lackeys to grow us a nice bed of catnip, and although I've suggested it several times, I haven't lost hope that one day it may happen."

"You might want to give up on that dream," the male responded, sulky that he had gotten it wrong. "After all, you have eaten at least three adventurers that have told you that the stuff won't grow in this climate."

The female harrumphed, and swished her thick tail this way and that in a great arc over the sand in frustration. "Tell the riddle to us again." she requested impatiently.

Over the course of the next few hours, Harmonium had to retell his riddle another seven times as the large felines pondered, answered, and proved to each other why their guesses were no good. Finally, as the orange and yellow sun was slowly falling toward the horizon, the male cat shouted "Pie! The answer is *pie*."

"Well now, that's just ridiculous!" the female informed him before he could even begin to look proud of himself. When have you ever seen a pie as small as a flea? How could someone even cook one that small? Or the opposite, when was the last time you saw a pie as big as one of us?"

The male opened his mouth to answer, but she cut him off, "Besides the ones in your dreams." His mouth snapped shut.

"Wait, that's it! A *dream*! I'm right, aren't I, monk?" The female didn't shoot down his answer right away, so he started going through all the clues. "A dream can be big or small. Adults and children have tried to keep their dreams alive. They don't have faces or bodies and they can be old or new."

The female began shaking her head. "How can you give a dream away? Besides, the clue was that adults and children have tried to keep it, not keep it *alive*. It still doesn't fit, but I think you may be on to something."

Sometime in the afternoon, Harmonium had grown weary of standing, and had seated himself in the warm sand. Noticing the look of superiority on the female's face, he now stood up.

"I have solved it," the female sphinx gloated. "The answer is a *secret*, is it not?"

Harmonium began brushing at the sand that stuck to his billowy pants. He donned his backpack and answered her. "It is," he said simply, "and now, I am ready to go."

"I hope you don't intend to eat the wee one all by yourself." the male cat grumbled.

"Why shouldn't I? I was the one who solved the riddle." she reminded him.

"Actually," Harmonium interrupted, "you have lost our wager, so Wolfbane is no longer yours to fight over."

"I earned that snack!" the female snarled at the monk in an earth rumbling growl.

Though the ground under his feet seemed to shake, Harmonium remained unruffled. "Cast your eyes above," he instructed.

Looking up, the sphinxes realized to their astonishment, that the sun had been replaced by the first splash of stars across the darkening evening sky.

The female made no move to back down. Instead, she bounded up into the sky and unfurled her wings to take to flight. She circled over the pyramid once, and sped off to the west.

"Quickly, we must follow her," the male let him know apologetically. "She was ever the sore loser. I'm afraid that your friend might be gone by the time we arrive if we don't take wing this second."

Harmonium didn't comment. He scrambled up the cat's leg by grabbing fistfuls of the sphinxes fur one after another until he had reached the giant cat's neck. The sphinx crouched with lightning fast reflexes, and before Harmonium could properly situate himself, the cat was in the air soaring after his mate.

* * *

Lazelan and Harmonium had taken a break from their hours of walking. They had supped on rations they carried in their backpacks; a gift from Xinavane, the princess of the Embralish desert people that they had left earlier that day. As they watched the sun near the horizon, however, both men had wordlessly returned to their feet and had continued trudging through the sand toward greener land. Lazelan had refused to use a light spell, reasoning that the beam would act as a beacon that would draw the sphinxes right to them in the dusk. Without light, they would be harder to find. Of course, it also meant that their progress was a good deal slower.

It wasn't long before they heard a cat's hiss, and the flapping of mighty feathered wings. Wolfbane looked toward the sound and fell face-first into the sand as he misjudged a step over the crest of another dune. He slid on his stomach for three feet, the sand cascading down around him as he went.

"We can't hide, I'll just wait here for the inevitable." he decided dejectedly. "I should have known that they'd sort out the answer. I guess a part of me had a bit of faith that the mage might actually come through for me."

"Night has fallen, but with an aggressive sound like that, I'm guessing that the sphinxes aren't going to keep up their end of the bargain. Still, you're not going to die today." Lazelan declared roughly, "Now, get up and fight, here it comes!"

Lazelan began to clear his mind, and channel his energy in preparation of his first spell. He pushed his hands out toward the oncoming feline and cried, "Kaeja nula kaez!" *Gust of wind.*

The feline caterwauled unexpectedly as the gust caught her wings, throwing her up into the night. It didn't take long for her to recover though, and unfortunately, the spell had missed the second cat that was catching up quickly at a lower altitude and had avoided the gust. The male sphinx never stopped, it only drew closer. To Lazelan, it appeared as if the cat was growing as it came. The female ended up using the extra height to her advantage and threw herself into a dive aimed directly at Wolfbane.

To his credit, the gnome got to his feet. He seemed to have come to terms with what was going to happen, and he was ready to face it head on. The giant sphinx slammed into the dune in front of them, sending a wave of sand into their faces, blinding both the human and the gnome. In the same instant, the second cat landed behind the first, and made to swipe at the sphinx in front of him. In a blind last ditch effort to preserve his life, Wolfbane went for his scimitar. The blade blazed to life as he drew it from the scabbard, the fire lighting the sky almost as brightly as a sun.

Both sphinxes gasped and halted.

As Lazelan blinked more and more sand out of his eyes, Lazelan's vision returned. What he witnessed to his sheer disbelief, was the gigantic cats laying prostrate to the gnome on the ground in front of him. The female apologized to Wolfbane for almost eating him, and practically begged him to choose her to ride to wherever he wanted to go.

Minutes later, while the male sphinx carried Lazelan and Harmonium in the lead, it spoke to the monk, beginning to work it out.

"You knew all along," the cat stated to the mage.

"I strongly suspected." Harmonium allowed.

"So this whole contest-," the sphinx realized,

"-Was a lesson in humility." Harmonium finished.

Feeling completely lost, Lazelan finally asked "But what made you so sure that the sphinxes would stop?"

Both Harmonium and the half-cat answered together: "Jarusiyat." *Chosen.*

"The gnome's blade of fire is an omen." The sphinx told the mage, "He is the Chosen One."

Lazelan knew that the Embralish people's society was based on omens, and the honour of being chosen to serve their princess, Xinnavane. But he hadn't suspected that those ideals would have spilled out of the pyramid to the sphinxes that had guarded it. He worried about the gnome though, whose mouth sometimes had a way of running away on him. Lazelan wondered just how far Wolfbane would be able to push the idea of being Jarusiat before the sphinxes might have enough. Not only that, but Lazelan strongly suspected that the farther they got from the Embralic Desert, the easier it would be for the giant man-eating cats to forget.

●

Chapter 3
O Beginning to See the Light O

Sasha lay once again on her grand bed, this time in the middle of the day. She and the queen had sat up for quite some time in the wee hours of the morning to talk about the stresses they had both been feeling over the tea and chicken. It had been a relief to have been able to confide in someone, and with her friend's reassurances, she felt more confident that things would once again right themselves if she just kept trying. It was at times like these that Sasha was thankful for the life of a noble that the previous king had afforded her, and that she had now grown accustomed to living. It gave her certain allowances, like being able to take a nap whenever she chose. After the middle-of-the-night visit, sleep would be heaven, whether it brought to her any foretelling visions or not.

She closed her eyes, thinking about the queen's casting problems. She needed a topic to focus on, and this was as good as any. Brightness be willing, she may even get a vision that would help them deal with the issue. She began by going over all the information she had.

Aylan had been King Oslan's mage for years, and she was incredibly skilled at the job. The man who had taught her all she knew about magic was Lazelan, the mage who had served Oslan's father before leaving his post to marry and settle down. Although Lazelan was on a quest in another realm, he and Aylan had arranged times to scry each other so they could communicate. He had been trying to help her by encouraging her to go back to the basics. He had given her a couple of tasks to hone her skills and become more precise.

For at least two fortnights now, she had had problems with casting on a large scale. So now Lazelan was trying to help her pull back her power to become more exact. He reasoned that with less energy going into the spell, there would be less that could go wrong.

Yesterday had found the queen once again confined to her bed as she had watched her lady-in-waiting, Millie, arrange ten candles on a brazier. They were all a similar shade of pleasantly-smelling off-white beeswax, save for one that was made of stinky yellow tallow. Although lighting them all with one spell directed at the brazier was normally easy for her, Lazelan had given her the task of trying to make only a small flame come to life on the one made of tallow, leaving the rest unlit.

The queen had been brimming with frustration as she had told Sasha about how she hadn't been able to complete Lazelan's task even once. She was convinced that her magic seemed to be broken. It was going haywire as of late to the point that even she was becoming wary of using her gift at all. She felt that she couldn't rely on it. All that afternoon and late into the evening, no matter how hard she had concentrated at the wicks, not a single flame had been produced. In fact, each time she had attempted to cast the fire spell, the shield she had been trying to cast previously had sprung up instead.

After trying all night, she had given up close to tears. The queen had stormed out of her chambers in a less than regal quick waddle with one hand supporting the aching small of her back. She had been walking aimlessly down the hall, trying to put magic as far from her mind as possible, when all of the torches on the wall sprung to life as she swayed by each one. By the time she ran into Sabyn fetching Sasha's tea, she had become suddenly ravenous, and had needed to sit down. The sight of her friend's handmaid had given her direction, and she toddled off toward the rooms the seer kept. The torches had continued to ignite with no help from her, but by the time she had arrived at the seer's door, so much of her energy had been drained that she couldn't have lit a candle if she had been so inclined to try.

As Sasha's busy mind replayed the stories that the queen had told her about the previous night, the seer's jaw began to slacken and her body relaxed. The ideas and focussed thoughts running through her mind began to meld into other things, and before too long, Sasha's even breathing and the occasional twitch of a slender finger denoted that she had begun to slumber.

She caught glimpses of a foreign land from a lofty perspective that was much too high to be human. Little snippets of countryside flew by before the darkness rolled over her dreams, blocking them out. In her sleep, Sasha's brow furrowed and then smoothed out as another flash of unfamiliar terrain passed under her. Snippets of conversation came to her with each moment of clarity. Dark blue-green waves with white caps rolled in a continual rising and falling motion as three male voices discussed a race of beings that purportedly lived under the water. The next flash of scenery was familiar. To her surprise, Endalwynndale's farmland appeared, and a voice that she knew well said "We're almost there."

The last part of her dream presented her with a magnificent view of the castle from up among the clouds. As the picture slowly spun, a volley of small black dots appeared. The men yelled, but Sasha could feel the vision slipping away. She clawed at the dream, trying desperately to stay within its story, needing to know more. Once again, the blackness passed over what had become a nightmare. In a last fleeting second of sight, she saw that the specks had grown to become deadly arrows. Her ears were filled with the pained roar of a lion and the scream of the voice that she had recognized as Lazelan's. The world abruptly spun and the castle suddenly began to rush at her at a blinding speed.

●

Chapter 4
O Hold On O

The blackness came in the nick of time, and Sasha's eyes flew open to see that she was sitting bolt upright in her bed. Tears streamed down her pale cheeks. She found her handmaid staring at her anxiously.

"Sabyn, we have to get to the queen!"

*   *   *

Aylan's mother, Lorelyn, sat at the wooden table beside the queen's large canopied bed. In front of her, a piece of parchment lay beside an inkpot. Her feather quill was poised above the paper as Aylan read out a list of names.

"So far we have Athrusia, Thrushyn, Thrushlynn, Thrushal, and just plain old Thrush." She said.

"What about adding something to the beginning?" her mother suggested.

This was becoming a harder endeavour than Aylan had originally thought it would be. At their wedding, a decoration had been picked from a tree bursting to the brim with all sorts of ornaments. On the one that had been chosen, had been a picture of a bird done in a young child's attempt at embroidery. Whoever had made the decoration was supposed to step forward to give their name to the couple. A young girl had come forth and had given the name *Thrush*. According to the customs of the people of Endalwynndale, it would become part of the name of the family's first born child. The only problem that Aylan was having was that it was clearly a boy's name, and yet she wondered what they would call the baby if it turned out to be a girl.

It was common for folk to make a new name derived from the one chosen, and that is what Lorelyn was trying to help her with as they visited over a stomach-calming tisane.

"Althruna?" the queen tried.

Lorelyn added it to the list. "What about something like Sarthrush?" she suggested.

The queen nodded for her to add it to the list, but she sighed. Nothing had sounded just right, and for some reason, she had a feeling of certainty that her baby was going to be a girl. Aylan's stomach began to unsettle again, and she grimaced. She needed some ginger.

Millie, who had been silently doing some mending in the corner, caught the expression of unease that crossed the queen's usually beautiful face. She quickly set down the dress she had been working on, and took up a fairly large lidded clay pot. With the queen's continued sickness, she was on duty to clean it out whenever Aylan's stomach made a deposit. But this time, the queen waved her off.

"It's not that bad this time, I just need some tea." Aylan assured her.

Millie carried the pot over to Lorelyn and set it on the ground out of the way.

"I will go fetch you some dry toast. That should also help." her lady-in-waiting told her before slipping out the door.

With Millie temporarily gone, that left Aylan to her own devices to reach the tea that sat on a serving tray on the coverlet of the bed where Aylan couldn't kick it by accident. The queen leaned forward, trying to keep her chin up so her straight blonde hair wouldn't fall in her face as she reached for her cup. She couldn't quite make it, her belly prevented it. She reached a little further, but it was no good. Her mother started to rise, but the queen stubbornly insisted, "I can reach it!" as her outstretched hand opened and shut desperately like a crab's pincers, as if that could help her get any further.

"Don't be silly." Her mother scolded her as she crossed the few steps between them and easily picked up the cup.

It was then that Sasha burst in without so much as a knock. Her normally unblemished creamy complexion was overly pale, save for some rosy spots on her cheeks from her exertions to get here.

"We must act quickly, Your Majesty!" she implored her friend. "Something is coming, and Lazelan is in danger. I had a vision. It was all bits and pieces, but I think he might be riding some sort of beast. Ormond is going to send the archers to their posts, but we can't let him, they are going to shoot him out of the sky! We must get Oslan to meet with the general immediately."

Horrified, Aylan started turning her body so she could leave the bed. "Oslan is still away hunting. We'll have to stop the archers ourselves. Quickly, Mother, bring my dressing gown!"

Lorelyn was throwing the robe around her daughter when something large momentarily blocked out the light by flying between Aylan's window and the sun. Then it was gone and the room was left bright again. The three ladies heard terrified screams and shouts to find cover coming from the marketplace below. They ran to the windows to look out and saw peasants fleeing the streets of the market. Most merchants had left their wares unattended as they also ran to find some kind of shelter, but from what, they didn't know. Then, as they watched the shutters closing one by one on the buildings below, a huge shadow briefly raced across the ground. It was long and lean, with the outline of feathery wings and a long slender tufted tail.

The door banged open and Millie rushed inside clutching a tray of toast to her chest. She slammed the door shut behind her, leaning on it as if she could hold it closed against whatever was out there. She looked to be in a sorry state. Her hair was mussed and she panted as if she had run across the whole castle. Realizing that she still held the queen's food, she crossed the room and hastily put it on the table. A piece of the toast stuck fast to her bodice, held there by a dollop of jam. She looked at the queen, who pulled the toast off of her dress and took it with her as she kept waddling steadily toward the door. There was work to do, but she was still hungry. She could eat on the way. The handmaid moved quickly and tried to put herself between her ruler and the door.

"Milady, it's pandemonium out there, we have to hide you!" she cried in a panic. Desperately looking around the room for a place that would conceal the queen, she finally settled on the room's centerpiece. "Quick, Milady, under the bed!"

"Step aside, Millie, I have to get to Ormond before the archers get their orders to shoot.

Lorelyn, who was still watching at the window, called out "We need to go now, the knights and knights-in-training are all pouring out of the barracks in full gear. They're already on their way, and the archers have their bows and quivers."

It seemed to be taking forever for Aylan to be able to get anywhere, as encumbered as she was with the baby. Sasha was fraught with worry that they weren't going to make it in time.

"I'm going to run ahead and see if I can find them. They'll likely be taking position on the battlements."

Sasha ran to the nearest tower and started her ascent up the spiral staircase to the door at the top of the curtain wall. On the far end stood Ormond in all of his knightly glory, with archers three deep lined up to shoot. Looking up, she saw something dark swoop overhead, obstructing the sun just like the eclipses in her dreams. It left her with a sense of vertigo until she shut her eyes against the world and let her mind settle. Opening her light-brown eyes once again, she tried to race the rest of the way to the general.

"Sir Ormond, you must stop!" she tried to yell over the clatter of men talking, finding their places, and nocking their arrows. She watched in terror as the shadows made another pass over all of the men, and a few of the younger archers drew back on their bowstrings without being commanded to.

There was no way she could get to the general. The men were too thick in their numbers, and the wall too narrow to afford her any more room. She felt her throat begin to prickle and her vision began to swim again as tears began to well up in her eyes. This was hopeless, she needed a backup plan. Then she spied Thorn, Millie's younger brother. He was an archer as well, and was mercifully close by. She rushed to him and explained the situation to him as quickly as she could. He jumped into action immediately.

"Hold!" he bellowed at his fellow knights. "Stand down!"

To her relief, Sasha watched as the closest archers lowered their bows. As the next group saw what was happening, they too began to loosen their pull on their bowstrings. Thorn went down the line giving the new command over and over. Ormond saw what was happening and headed toward the scrawny teenager. Ormond finally got the message, and quickly set about to disarm the knights-in-training.

They normally would have never been put into action while still so new, but they had been called out because of the state of emergency the situation had created. They hadn't been put through their paces yet, they were still too green. But Ormond had seen this as a good training lesson.

The shadow came again as the queen finally joined them. Most of the knights returned their arrows to their quivers, took a knee, and gave her the salute, which guaranteed that they meant her no harm. However, one of the over-zealous young boys decided that he was going to be a hero.

"Don't worry, Your Majesty," his voice carried over the other men, "I won't let that monster get you!" he reassured her.

Ormond shouted for the boy to stop, but neither his menacing disposition, nor orders with the threats of repercussions were enough to hold the determined youth back.

He neatly raised his nocked arrow and drew back on his bowstring, aiming at the monster's heart.

Chapter 5
O Not in the Cards O

Odal Strongaxe sat in the tavern of the sapphire clan deep in the heart of Mount Embalk. The walls glittered with the veins of blue that ran through this cavern. All of the corridors that housed the dwarves had been smoothed and polished and made pleasant for them to inhabit. A sturdy maid came to the table to bring the five heads of the clans their mugs of stout dwarven ale. Odal looked up at the maid to thank her and noticed her piercing green eyes and luxurious long reddish beard. She had woven little blue flowers into the braids of her whiskers. They looked very becoming.

"Thank you." He said gruffly and went back to his game. He never had been very good at talking to attractive women. Humans and elven ladies he had no problems talking to; they were too tall, thin, and had hairless chins. They gave him the willies. That was all fine though, because it made him a good ambassador for his clan when they travelled outside the mountain to other towns.

Odal sat looking at his cards and tried not to let the expression on his face give anything away. He briefly looked up at the other four dwarves to see what their visages might reveal. *Nothing.* He was going to have to do this the hard way, by depending on pure dumb luck.

Three of the other players had already laid down a set to declare for a house. Durlak sat with three cards bearing a picture of a sapphire on the table in front of him. Azagut had declared for the emerald house, and Dain had already collected and laid down five amethysts. Nalvo sat as Odal did, with nothing yet on the table. Odal didn't trust Nalvo as far as he could jump, though given his sturdy and husky size, that wouldn't have been very far to begin with.

Azagut sighed loudly, voicing that he was tired of waiting for Odal to make a move. But the dwarf had a decision to make. In his hand he held two cards with glinting rubies on them, and another pair showing beautifully striped tigers-eye gems. His fifth card bore a mask for a masquerade, he could use it to represent any gem he chose. He needed to declare for a house by putting at least three cards of the same jewel on the table, but once he did, he couldn't switch. On the one hand, the top card on the discard pile showed a gleaming tigers-eye ripe for the taking. However, Odal remembered seeing more than one other gem of brown, yellow, and gold discarded further down. Without a mage card, it would be hard to recapture either to add to his house. He ran his thick fingers and thumb down over his wiry brownish-red beard. He often did this when he had a decision to make. It helped him think.

Nalvo's elbow caught the edge of an empty mug that had been inconveniently left at the side of the table, sending it clattering onto the floor. Odal noticed that as Nalvo bent to the side to retrieve it, his eyes got a good long look at Durlak's cards.

"Durlak, guard your cards." Odal warned. As Nalvo righted himself and replaced the mug on the large round table, he glared at Odal.

"Are you going to make your move? I think my beard is starting to come in grey." Nalvo sneered, fingering his blond whiskers.

"I might not be very fast, but at least I don't cheat." Odal muttered under his breath.

"What was that?" Nalvo challenged immediately.

"I said that I think this round has me beat." Odal covered up smoothly. "I declare for house ruby," he stated, finally making his decision. He discarded the tigers-eyes and reached for the deck to refresh his hand. He came away with another ruby and the mage card. Inside, he rejoiced. Outwardly, his face was as unchanging as the stone walls of the cave around them.

Kingdom had been invented by a traveller that had visited the dwarven cities and had been inspired by the shining jewels that coloured the walls of the caves. Each clan mined a different type of gemstone, and their halls had been carved out of an area that held those veins. If one were to visit with Durlak's clan, they would find the smoothly polished walls of the hallways and large caves to have what appeared to be endless shimmering rivers of rubies that made glossy swirling patterns of the gem that were a wonder to behold. It was the same for every inch of Mount Embalk that the dwarves inhabited.

Kingdom represented each of the six clans; diamond, sapphire, emerald, tigers-eye, amethyst, and of course, ruby. It was a game widely played among the dwarves. This particular sitting had a bet riding on it, though it was not actually a game meant for gambling. It had just seemed like the easiest way to settle a decision that the five of them were trying to hash out.

Aside from the six veins of precious rock, each with their own system of hallways and caverns, there was one central great hall with a vaulted ceiling so high that all of the gemstones merged together colouring its walls in all of the hues like the inside of an opal. This was the most impressive cavern in the whole mountain, and it was used to hold meetings that involved more than one clan. It was also the most sought after for members to claim for feasts, or celebrations such coming-of-age ceremonies or weddings. This was the conundrum that the dwarves were finding themselves in now. Agamm Earthdig, leader of the diamond clan, had a daughter that was scheduled to get married in the multi-coloured hall. They had booked the hall over a year in advance when the young dwarven couple had become betrothed. Unfortunately, it was also the same night as the yule feast that all of the clans participated in. Therefore, all of the other clan chiefs were vying for whose halls would host the festival this year since the grand hall was already spoken for.

After a few more turns, Odal found himself frowning down at the table. Azagut seemed to be winning. He was also smiling smugly. The head of the Amethyst clan had already laid down nine of the eleven emerald cards that he would need to win. Odal looked at his own hand and saw that he was holding the emerald king that his companion would need. Odal felt like giving him a comfortable grin of his own, but crushed the urge. The smile on Azagut's face faded, and his brow furrowed in consternation. *Drat,* Odal mentally cursed. One of his features must have given it away. It could have been the twitch of an eye or the slight lifting of the corner of the mouth. The problem with playing cards with your closest friends was that you got to know each other's tells quite quickly if you liked to win, and they all did. Either way, as long as Odal held onto that baker, Azagut couldn't collect all eleven types of subjects he would need to complete his clan and win the kingdom. Odal decided that he would hold onto it for the rest of the game. This wouldn't guarantee his victory, but at least he wouldn't have to celebrate in a glitzy purple hall;

purple was his least favourite colour. Then again, anything would be better than having Nalvo win. He was so dishonest that he'd probably brag about serving his guests prime rib, but end up just giving them rump roast.

It wasn't long before the game appeared to be tied, and it came around to Odal's turn again. He hoped that he would draw one of the last three rubies that he would need. All that remained to be found were the child, bard, and the queen.

He played the seer card and heard two of his friends groan. The sound of their angst made him giddy. They had every reason to be worried at this point in the game. He could almost taste victory. This card gave him the ability to pick up the four top cards on the deck. He could take one if there were any ruby subjects to be had. Equally as great though, was the power to take the rest and then rearrange them in any order he saw fit before returning them to the top or bottom of the deck. He now had the power to decide for the next couple of turns, what his buddies would get. His grin reached from ear to ear.

Mentally, he began to make preparations for the big event. He would have to bring in some kegs of ale, and send out a hunting party down the mountain to bring back at least three moose or elk worthy of a feast for all the clans. He would have to hold auditions for the few bards among the clan to provide entertainment. Well, who was he kidding? He already had a favourite. He liked Garngal Highnote, of the sapphire clan, and his songs about the confused maiden from Evelynton. Odal would have to find out how much he charged.

Dain cleared his throat and Odal was reminded that he was in the middle of his turn. He peeked at the top corner of the first card and felt his sense of hope deflate when he saw that there was no gleam of red in the corner. His disappointment was brief though, and he soon found himself overjoyed at finding a ruby on the second. His heart leapt into his throat when he saw the last two that he had drawn. He held in his hand two of the three cards he still needed. However, he was only allowed to keep one. He hastily took the child card and placed it on the table in order with the others in his laid down clan. For the other three, including his needed queen, he would have to return them to the deck. He could still get it back when he picked up at the end of his turn, which made him want to dance.

Now I will just need the bard. This was the trickiest part of the game. He thought about the emerald in his hand, and eyed the other players at the table. The only thing he could do now was to watch his friends draw, and decide which of his opponents would get his last card and hold it against him.

Chapter 6
O Worth A Shot O

Aylan did the only thing that she could think of as the insolent boy took aim at the giant flying cat that carried Lazelan. She cleared her emotions and tried to concentrate on a single act. She could feel the magic draining some of her energy to complete the spell, but nothing seemed to be happening. She had attempted to cast a shield on the giant cat, but it wasn't working. It shouldn't matter that the sphinx was flying around, she had once helped her former teacher safely dispose of some sky fire packets that an evil mage had try to harm the people of the kingdom with during a display. Those had been little, and she had had no trouble. This cat was the size of a blooming barn! How could she have missed?

She felt like she wanted to cry out of frustration. This was happening more and more frequently. Her mother had told her that that was normal during a pregnancy. Lorelyn had warned that her emotions would run like a kite; soaring and plummeting, turning this way and that for what appeared to be no good reason. She had said that it would be hard to bring them back in check, and that that was alright.

Lazelan hadn't noticed the lone archer that hadn't dropped his bow, but the sphinx had. The cat's body tilted, spilling Lazelan and Harmonium to the side. They both screamed and grabbed handfuls of fur to holding on for dear life. The cat began a banking turn, but now it's belly was exposed and neither mage could see what was happening below.

It had to be her. Blinking back the hot tears before they could fall, Aylan unclenched the fists her hands had seemed to have formed and focussed again. She tried to cast her spell again, this time raising her hand toward the cat and saying the spell aloud instead of in her head.

"Falfakti!" *Shield!* Staring at the cat incredulously, she still saw no obvious effect. However behind her she heard a squeak. She turned and saw that the knight behind her was surrounded by a thin glowing blue layer of protection.

"Arg!" she fumed out of desperation and frustration. She could feel herself weakening with each used effort. She had enough energy left for maybe one more attempt. She said a quick prayer to the brightness that surrounded them for aid or for luck. Her legs buckled as she drained the rest of her energy and sent forth the burst of magic.

Having carefully taken aim, the archer blew out a steady breath and let his fingers loosen on the bowstring. As his grip let go and the string pushed the arrow forward, the torch on the merlon beside the boy burst into flame, scorching his arm. The boy dropped his bow as the fight of his arrow passed the bent arc of wood.

It had been just enough. The shot flew wild, going over the outer curtain wall, and burying itself among the needles at the top of an evergreen tree.

The queen lay safely in the arms of the three closest knights, who had lunged in to catch her before she could hit the ground. Ormond ordered one of them to take her back to her chambers, and Sasha offered to go with him to make sure that she was alright. Although the crisis had been averted for now, there were still the beautiful winged beasts to contend with.

Sasha led the knight to the queen's chambers and opened the door for him. They found Millie still in the room with Lorelyn. Both positioned themselves at one of the windows so they could keep appraised of the situation. Since they were still watching as intently as a child at a puppet show, it appeared as though they hadn't seen the queen fall.

When Lorelyn saw Aylan dangling limply from the knight's arms, she rushed over and helped him get her onto the bed.

"Quick, fetch a cold cloth, just over there." she instructed Millie.

"I will get her smelling salts, too," Sasha declared, and left the knight to tell Lorelyn what had conspired on the part of the battlement that wasn't visible from Aylan's window.

As the knight explained what he had seen, Millie poured water from the pitcher as she held a cloth over the wash basin. Setting the pitcher down, she rang out the cloth and returned to Lorelyn's side, handing it over. As Lorelyn dabbed at Aylan's forehead, one of the beasts flew close by the chamber windows. They caught a glimpse of giant claws and sand-coloured fur before it was gone again.

Sasha ran down the corridor to the hall that held the armoury. The two guards that were posted there recognized her at once, although they had never seen her rush in anything less than a ladylike fashion. Right now, she was outright running with her skirts flying, and she wasn't prepared to stop.

"Open the door!" she ordered breathlessly as she closed the distance to the entryway. The guard on the right barely moved fast enough, but managed to get the heavy oak door to swing inward just as Sasha rounded the door jam. "Thank you!" she called out over her shoulder as she continued past the suits of armour, swords, shields, bows, and other matter of defense. She passed through the door on the opposite end of the room, which let her into the empty war room. She skirted the huge heavy table, and moved to the end of the floor-to-ceiling tapestry that depicted the whole kingdom.

She paused long enough to snatch a candle off the table, fasten it in a candlestick holder, and took the time to light it. Then carefully keeping the flame away from the tapestry, she pulled back the edge of the impressive woven wall hanging and slipped behind it into a secret passage that only a handful of people knew about.

Chapter 7
O Calling the Kettle Black O

The truth was that Odal didn't actually want to win. As dwarves go, he was the lazy sort. Winning would mean having to do all that actual preparation that he had been dreaming up in his head. Thinking about something was one thing, it took no effort. But actually doing it, well, that was another story completely. He had gotten so good at being lazy that most of his clan members didn't even bother him with the little stuff. They now took it upon themselves to get things done because they would do it in a timelier manner. But he was an incredible idea man. That's how he had been elected as the chief to represent the tigers-eye clan. He was very good at coming up with solutions to problems, even if he was slow to act on them himself.

When it came to this game, he could take or lose whether he won or not. But what he did care about, what he was *concerned* about, was who else might win in his place. His first choice would have been the diamond clan, as anything went with diamonds and Agamm always threw a good party. However, since red-bearded dwarf would be at his daughter's wedding, the obvious choice was out. Odal didn't think that he could bear it if Azagut or Nalvo were to win, and that left only Dain or Durlak to choose from.

He looked in his hand at the three remaining cards he had yet to return to the deck. He had none of the ones that Dain was collecting, and even if he had, with the black-haired dwarf sitting to his right, it wouldn't have helped. But Odal did have one of the two cards that Durlak was searching for, and he was going to be drawing next.

Odal put the cards back on the top of the deck in order so that he would pick up the other ruby and tigers-eye. Then Durlak would get the sapphire he needed. He discarded, drew his two, and sat back satisfied that he had done his best. He looked at his friends and took a significant gulp of his ale.

Durlak played a thief card, making Dain lose one of the cards he had already laid on the table. Then Durlak discarded and drew two cards off the deck. His bushy eyebrows shot up in surprise. Odal caught the other dwarf looking at him as if to ask if he had meant to do that, and tried to ignore him by burying himself in another drink before the others would notice. Durlak would never be good at this game until he learned to guard his face. To Odal's surprise though, Durlak didn't play the card he had picked up, so the others still wouldn't necessarily know what Odal had left him.

Then it was Nalvo's turn. He still needed four more subjects for his clan, so Odal wasn't overly worried. He started by laying a traveller card, which let him use a different gem in place of his own. *Drat! He only needs three more now. This game is getting too close,* Odal silently sulked.

With his next card, Nalvo played a falcon directed at Odal. This would force Odal to hand over a diamond that Nalvo needed if the other dwarf had held one. Odal didn't, and apologetically told Nalvo so with a jovial grin that somewhat soured the apology. Perhaps it wasn't always necessary to hide one's feelings at the table. Sometimes, the joy just seemed to come out on its own.

Now, Nalvo could randomly choose a card out of Odal's hand. Odal, hoped that the blond dwarf wouldn't manage to choose one of the event cards that Odal had planned on using. Those were the game changers. Nalvo reached across the table, waved his hand over Odal's fanned out cards, and pulled one out. Odal almost laughed when the other dwarf took the worthless tigers-eye card from his hand. He suppressed the urge with some difficulty though, and signaled the serving girl instead.

To his credit, Nalvo had mastered hiding what he was really feeling, probably due to the almost compulsive lying that he did. He never so much as grimaced when he picked out the tigers-eye, but he was a cunning dwarf, and had probably expected no favours from Odal's hand in the first place.

Nalvo eyed Dain for a moment, picking at the corner of one of his cards. He smiled and played the mage. Dain sat up straight at the sight of it. He was a chieftain, but he was a real mage as well. This was his favourite card, for obvious reasons. This one allowed Nalvo to look back through the discard pile until he came to one of the diamonds he needed, which he could then take.

Drat, thought Odal, *he's one card closer. Only two left to go. He just* can't *win!*

Nalvo grabbed up the discard pile and began rifling through it with glee. He pulled a diamond out with a flourish, added it to his hand, and put the rest back. He was making ready to lay the card that he had just pulled when Yili, the server whose beard was adorned with the blue flowers, passed the table carrying a tray of mugs. As she swaggered behind Nalvo, she seemed to accidently knock his elbow with her hip, sending his cards sprawling on the floor. They all landed face down, and with an unkind word for the pretty girl, Nalvo bent down to pick up his cards. This time, Durlak was ready for him, and held his own cards close to his chest so they could not be observed.

Nalvo straightened in his seat, and sniffed as if to say that he was offended that Durlak's posture had insinuated that he would try to peek. He still had the chance to lay down the card that he had just captured. He looked at the three cards in his hand and laid them all down.

"I win." He stated smugly.

Odal sat in stunned silence for a moment. His mind couldn't wrap itself around what had just happened.

"What kind of game is this?" He challenged angrily, staring at the three freshly played diamonds that lay there.

"Oh, Odal, you know that we were playing Kingdom, what kind of question is that? I think you've had enough ale, my friend." With that declaration, Nalvo stood, and told the others that he would be looking forward to seeing them at the yule feast that would be held within the sapphire hall.

"Normally I would tell you to sit down Nalvo, and I would tell the others that we still had a right and proper game to finish. But, I have no urge to keep playing with a cheater." Odal said blatantly.

Durlak's snowy white hair fell forward as he planted his gnarled fists on the table and stood. "What's the meaning of this?" he demanded in his rickety old man's voice. The soft rabbit fur that lined his robe had been dyed a deep red to symbolize the ruby clan that he represented. The dark crimson seemed to add an element to the anger he was displaying, making it seem all the more fierce.

"I don't know," Nalvo said, feigning innocence, "I picked out the cards I needed, that is all. Obviously Odal is confused, or he's a sore loser and is trying to cheat."

"I'm not confused, and I'm certainly not cheating!" Odal roared, "The card you drew from my hand was the blacksmith of tigers-eye, it was no diamond!"

"Are you sure, Odal?" Durlak asked.

"Yes, I'm positive. You all know me; I would never make a mistake like that."

"There is an easy way to discover the truth," Dain said calmly. "Durlak, if you wouldn't mind putting all of the cards back in the box."

All of the players that still held cards in their hands threw them onto the pile. Durlak collected them all and placed the deck into its box, shutting the lid. Dain raised two hands out in front of him like he was a grandmother waiting for a young dwarf's hug. Then he said, "Ey niveani so vutmai nula akmaoae-ert vil!" *I summon the baker of tigers-eyes card.*

All of a sudden there was a papery fluttering that everyone could hear. Nalvo looked shocked, and quickly clamped his hand down on his opposite arm. He seemed to be struggling a bit as his straight arm seemed to want to rise. It began to shake, and he was exerting so much energy in trying to keep it down, that he was beginning to break a sweat. Finally after about ten agonizing seconds, his arm shot forward and a card flew out of his sleeve like the tongue of a frog coming out to catch a fly. The card flew to rest in Dain's palm, face down. Dain looked around at the anxious faces of the other dwarves and flipped it over. There in his palm sat the blacksmith of tigers-eye.

Chapter 8
O Salty Dog O

Sasha travelled by the dim light of the candle down the stone hallway, ducking under cobwebs that always seemed to reform no matter how many times Aylan cleared them away. Although Sasha had been here many times while Lazelan had been putting Aylan through her training, she didn't like the narrow passage. Just the windowless close proximity of the walls made her feel as if they were going to close in on her. She began to feel unsettled; it was getting harder for her to breathe, and not just because the air tasted stale. It felt like her insides were beginning to lock up, her lungs unwilling to take that next breath. She began to gasp. This was always worse when she was on her own. At least when she was with someone else, their conversation helped to take her mind off it. She unconsciously sped up her pace as she untrustingly eyed the unmovable stone.

She came to a set of stairs and knew that she was almost there. She lifted her dress so she wouldn't step on her gown while going up, and took them two at a time. She would have never done this in the presence of anyone else, but the speed and vertical rush was exhilarating. It also briefly gave her something to think about besides the tiny space that she was travelling through.

Closer now, she started to picture the vial that she was going to be looking for. In this case, she was lucky. It had a distinctive decoration, so it wouldn't look like the other vials or boxes. Aylan's workroom was not your average work space. It was actually a laboratory where she spent her time creating potions, pastes, powders, and pills using the art of herbology. Every vial, package, or flask in Aylan's laboratory was neatly labelled in her flowing script, but between the ingredients and remedies lining the wall of shelves, there were hundreds of containers that she would normally have to look through to find what she was looking for.

Travellers often gifted the king and queen with things when they came to visit the kingdom. Knowing that the queen was also a very talented herbologist meant that a great deal of these offerings were substances that were considered to be precious in Endalwynndale because they couldn't be found within the kingdom. Sasha knew that Aylan treasured every one, and not only because the guests usually put their offerings in decorative boxes and ornamental bottles that no one else on this side of the Ocean of Empathy would have. It meant that the queen could produce cures and potions that would have otherwise been impossible to make here.

Sasha made it to the wooden door at the end of the passage, and entered the organized workroom. She set the candle on the small square table in the centre of the room, and approached the first shelf of vials. These ones were all similarly shaped; thin and round, with cork stoppers or wads of material in the top to hold the substances in. She moved on. Looking at the next shelf over, she saw an array of ornate wooden chests and boxes. These were not what she was looking for. On the next shelf sat the ornamental glassware that she sought. *And now I just have to find the one with a small yellow dog on it,* she reminded herself.

Her eyes flicked over the glass bowls, cups, jars, and bottles until she found a hinged glass box with a little yellow dog on the lid amid the other designs. She carefully lifted it with both hands and brought it to the table. She set it down beside the candle and lifted the lid. Inside, the box had been divided into two parts. On the right, on a bed of folded velvet to cushion it, was a small dark stoppered bottle which was too opaque to see through. On the left lay several little rolls of material, which were each synched and tied off with string at both ends. *This is the one with the smelling salts, now to get it back to Aylan.*

She carefully tucked the box under one arm, lifted the candle, and left the room. Walking back through the horrid passageway, she tried to focus on being careful with the box to keep her mind off of her unease at the enclosed space. The trip back out seemed quicker than on the way in, and she breathed a sigh of relief as she caught her first glimpse of the tapestry. She stopped just behind it and listened closely to make sure that no one had entered the war room. hearing no one, she slid out from behind the colossal work of stitched art.

She had not gotten two steps away from the woven reproduction of the kingdom when the sound of voices drew nearer and the door to the war room opened. Two of the king's knights entered, mid-conversation.

"-looked like someone was riding them!" the first one was saying. *What am I going to do?* the seer could feel panic rising at the possibility of getting caught without a real explanation of why she had come in here. She leashed it and thought quickly. Putting the candle down, she randomly grabbed one of the rolled up maps from the large table as if that had been her aim the whole time.

"Gentlemen," She greeted them smoothly, then dismissed herself with a brief nod of acknowledgement to the knights as she brushed past them and left through the armoury.

It didn't take her long to rush across the castle back to the royal chambers. Again without knocking, she rushed through the door. Tossing the map on the table, she went to the still unconscious queen. Lorelyn sat by the head of the bead, holding the damp cloth to her daughter's forehead. Millie stood close by looking very much like she wanted to have something to do. She was wringing her hands with worry as she helplessly looked on.

"Did you get them?" the lady-in-waiting asked anxiously.

"Yes, here they are." Sasha replied as she opened the box's lid to present them with the contents. She offered the box to Lorelyn, who took out one of the material cylinders, and held it under Aylan's nose. With a gasp, the queen's eyes flew open. Sasha was flooded by a sense of relief that her friend was alright. Lorelyn replaced the tiny roll, and Sasha set the box aside on the table with the map. She would have to remember to return both later.

"It worked!" Millie rejoiced, "Oh, Milady, we were so worried about you!" she gushed.

Aylan put one hand to her head as if she had a headache and the other to her belly as if to make sure that her baby was still there.

"I am fine now, I assure you. I just-"

She was interrupted by a hideous scraping noise that made Sasha's spine tingle in an awful way. It had come from above them. *Something just hit the roof!* she realized. Another series of clacks and the same horrid scraping sounds came from above, followed by a heavy *crack*. Millie ran to the window and attempted to look out and up. She drew her head rapidly back in as something slid down the side of the conical roof on the tower, fell past the window, and shattered on the cobblestones below.

"Are we under attack?" Aylan asked, flinging the covers back and turning to once again rise from her bed.

"I don't believe so, dear," her mother reassured her, but the look of unease on her face didn't really mesh with the message that she was trying to convey. "Back in bed," she ordered, tucking Aylan's feet back under the covers.

"I haven't seen anything else," Sasha tried to reassure her half-heartedly, though she knew that her visions hadn't been complete as of late. She normally would have been sure, but now she could only make her best guess. "Either way though, you can't cast anymore today. You need to build up your energy again first. Not to do so would be taking a stupid risk. When you fell, I thought that you had actually gone and done it."

Everyone knew that Sasha was right. Those close to the queen knew that if a mage were to completely deplete the pool of energy he or she used to cast from, then it would never be able to replenish, and they would be left as a normal, powerless husk of the person they had once been.

"You have knights to protect you, and you have to let them do their job, darling." Lorelyn reminded her.

A heavy sound came from directly above them, and particles of mortar from between the stones that made up their ceiling reigned down around the women.

"That's it," Aylan declared, "I've at least got to go see what is going on. Oslan's not here right now, so I'm the only ruler of the kingdom around to deal with these issues."

Sasha knew that there would be no dissuading her, so she stepped forward to help support her friend, who still seemed to be slightly shaky as she got to her feet. They all went together, forming a protective party around the queen. As they walked out the door, the two knights positioned down the hallway saw them emerge and came to lend their aid.

"Perfect, now we will look more official. Take me to the roof!" the queen commanded.

Chapter 9
O Cooped Up O

The male sphinx had attempted to alight on the conical roof of the tower at the end of the west wing. The red clay tiles that lay in scale-like rows had been too sleek for him to grab onto, and he had begun to slide backward. Making a horrific din, his claws had begun to scramble on the smooth surfaces, ripping off some of the clay tiles, and splitting or shattering others. Lazelan winced as some of the tiles slid down the roof to the courtyard below. Luckily, the unexpected appearance of the two giant flying cats had caused a scare, so no one had been below to be injured.

As the giant cat's paw slipped, his shoulder dipped, causing the two mages that were riding him to fall to the side. Lazelan and Harmonium grabbed onto the thick sandy fur to hold on for dear life, pulling the hair of the already terrified sphinx, which made it yowl in surprise. Finally, it managed to wrap its two powerful front paws around the peak of the roof, like a pet cat grabbing at a scratching post. It sat there, panting, while trying to reposition its hind paws.

Wolfbane had a much easier landing, as the female cat daintily alighted on the flat top of the keep. As the big cat crouched down to allow her passenger to get off, she began to purr, satisfied with her superior performance.

The male sphinx was never going to be able to sidle over to the flat area where the female was without more undignified scrambling, so he flapped his strong wings twice, took off again, and came to land beside her. He lay flat on his tummy, less for the benefit of the men to get off, and more out of trauma. They didn't have anything like that in the desert, everything was covered in a fine layer of sand or was made out of great bricks, which were easy to grab onto. The female leaned over and gave him a couple of reassuring licks on his head for good measure while Lazelan and Harmonium hopped down. Other than the towers, the roof was fairly empty, except for a structure that served as a pigeon and chicken coop. Emanating from the barred windows came the gentle cooing and insistent clucking of the fowl within.

"After all that flying, I'm starved," the male sphinx grumbled.

"Lazelan," the gnome got his attention, "Do you think the king and queen would be overly upset if we ate one of their birds? I too, am famished."

The great cat let out a rumble of a laugh. "Do you have any idea how many chickens it would take to feed us? We usually dine on larger fare, like the occasional camel that will appear with a rider that fails to solve their riddle."

"And that's after eating the man," the female chimed in with a fond smile.

"Well, you might turn your noses up at free food, but I would never." Wolfbane testified. "Well, rarely. Not unless I suspected poison, and even then, if the food smelled succulent enough..." he let his voice trail off as he marched toward the chicken and pigeon coop.

"I wouldn't if I were you," Lazelan warned, "Those fowl belong to the king and queen."

"Oh, lighten up, Lazelan, it's just a bird. What are you, *chicken*?" Wolfbane asked, tucking his thumbs into his armpits and flapping his elbows like wings. He opened the door and a brown hen immediately came flapping and fluttering out amid a cloud of rogue feathers.

"There, you can have that one; we'll call it an appetizer." The gnome told the hungry sphinx as he went inside and turned, leaving his hand on the knob. "Is anyone else coming? I'm going to close this so we don't end up with any more *jail birds*." When no one moved aside from the impatient flick of the male sphinx's tail, the gnome shook his head and shut the door behind him.

The cat got up and stalked over to the coop, turned, and sat down directly in front of the door. Then he stretched out and lazily licked at the chicken that was pecking at the dry stones of the roof.

"You have trapped him in there," the female sphinx scolded. "He's the chosen one," she reminded him.

"I'm not causing him any injury. I just figured that it wouldn't hurt him to be left *cooped up* for a while."

"Well done," the female congratulated him.

Then from inside the hen house, the gnome began to shriek.

❭

Chapter 10
O Taming of the Shrewd O

Sasha followed Aylan and the others up the tower steps to the door that opened onto the roof. A sense of fear and foreboding had created a sick knot in the pit of her stomach. Outwardly, Sasha was the poised and perfect lady that she always presented herself to be, but internally she was a torrent of emotions.

Although she considered herself to have been lucky to have gotten the vision of Lazelan's potential demise, her dream had stopped there. They still didn't know how he had come to meet this creature, if it was sentient, if it was friendly, or if Lazelan was under duress. She also didn't know if he was alone. There were so many unanswered questions that she wished uneasily that she had answers for. She had only gotten those snippets thanks to whatever was blocking her power of insight, so she hadn't yet gotten a really good look at the beast, and didn't know what to expect.

They were almost to the door when they heard a voice beyond it begin to shriek. The knights took the lead and ran up the last couple of stone spiral steps. They drew their swords, the one asking if the other was ready, and threw open the door, bathing them all in light.

Sasha couldn't see anything but the backs of those ahead of her. As they filed out through the door, she was able to continue advancing up the last steps. *What am I thinking? I'm not armed, none of us are. The queen's magic is on the fritz, and even if it were working, her energy pool has been drained. What are we going to do?*

"Millie," Sasha whispered, getting the maid's attention. "Go to the training arena and tell General

Ormond where we are." Millie raced back down the stairs into the castle. Hopefully, she wouldn't be long. Going out onto the roof, an unexpected scene was unfolding before them.

The colossal cats were the first thing that caught Sasha's eye. One sat with its back to her, and the other was crouched in their direction, but had turned its face to the door of the aviary. From what she could tell, they looked like lions with very human faces, and both had a set of long feathery wings. Her heart tripped at the sight before it decided to keep beating. Then she noticed Lazelan and a second bald man were also turning to look anxiously to the door. Something behind it was the source of that high pitched squeal, and now there began the sound of thuds against the wood as if something much larger than a bird was trying to get out.

"Lazelan!" Sasha called in relief at seeing him alive and well. He looked in her direction, and smiled a goofy boyish grin. She watched as both men bowed deeply to the queen at Sasha's side. The cats turned too, and when the female noticed the men bowing, she too dipped her head out of respect. The male took a look at the throng of newcomers and licked his lips. Quick as a flash, the female's tail whipped through the air and caught the other sphinx upside the back of his fuzzy head. He glared at her, but also bowed his head in diffidence to the lady in the golden gown that they both assumed to be the queen.

All of this had only taken a couple of seconds, and Aylan strode toward the source of the the continued shrieks and pounding, tottering dangerously from side to side as she went. Meanwhile the male cat addressed Sasha, "Your Majesty, we are weary travellers, who have journeyed across desert and ocean. Could you spare us a small meal? What about this great waddling one? She's like a walking appetizer and a meal all wrapped up in one." He smiled a feral grin that didn't touch his squinting eyes in a way that made a chill run up the seer's spine. Sasha gasped at his remark, and Aylan stopped short in front of the sphinx and planted her fists on her hips in a confrontational way. The sphinx lowered his head and raised his rear haunches as if he were getting ready pounce, which cleared the way for the wooden door behind him to slam open. To add to Sasha's surprise, out walked a gnome carrying a teeny tiny pigeon.

"Oh look, everyone, it's just a baby!" he gushed, holding up the squab for them to see. Then he got a look at the queen and went on, "Oh look, there are *two*!"

Sasha raised a hand to her mouth to stifle a laugh at this peculiar little man. She only knew who he was through Aylan's scrying with Lazelan, but she liked him already.

He walked over to Aylan and bowed low at the waist, holding the peeping bird out to the side on his palm.

"You must be the almighty and quite talented mage we have been hearing about for weeks, Your Grace," he acknowledged her. "I am humbled to be in your considerable presence."

Then he straightened without waiting for a response and placed the bird delicately on the swell of the queen's belly. Aylan arched her eyebrow, but the gnome didn't hesitate. He immediately took a knee in front of the queen saying, "And this is for you, my little prince or princess. You will take great care of each other, I know it!"

Sasha thought that she would die laughing at each of his comments had she allowed herself to outwardly show her mirth. But the guards didn't find the exchange entertaining at all. In fact, as soon as the gnome had moved toward the queen with the squab, the knights had stepped forward, at the ready to act. The queen however, looked to Lazelan for guidance, and only found him standing with his face in his palm shaking his head slowly from side to side. She waved back the knights and spoke to Wolfbane instead.

"If that pigeon relieves itself on me, you will be washing out this gown by hand." the queen told him with an arched eyebrow.

"Now, now, Your Grace, is that any way to ad*dress* a man who has just handed over a gift?" Wolfbane asked defensively. The queen's eyebrow dropped, and one side of her mouth quirked up in an amused smile.

"Do you know how *foul* it is to try to chide a queen? Besides, I already owned the bird." The queen pointed out, "So it wasn't exactly a present."

Wolfbane blinked in surprise. For that matter, Sasha was suspicious herself. She wasn't sure if Aylan had meant that as a pun, foul for fowl, or if it was a simple coincidence.

"Not for you, your grace. I was clearly *present*ing the babe with the gift." Wolfbane reminded the queen.

"While I admit that you are truly *gift*ed with words, surely you must realize that I am not going to be spending the next few weeks moving about the castle with a bird on my belly!" Aylan objected.

"What, you can't *stomach* it? Personally, I think the little squab looks pretty comfy." he declared.

"Don't be a *bird*-brain! I order you to take it off right now!" She huffed dramatically.

"Of course, Your Grace." He said with a humble voice and another low bow. "I would have *off*ered long ago if I thought it was truly causing you any discomfort." he confessed, hastily scooping up the bird, which had nestled down and was now upset at being moved.

Lorelyn had kept her eyes on the two sphinxes this whole time, and took a step closer to her daughter. "How can you just stand here bantering on with this young man when that giant flying cat just threatened to eat you?" Lorelyn asked her daughter incredulously.

"I have heard worse, Mother," Aylan admitted, "and I suppose the sphinx asked a valid question, even if it wasn't explicitly polite to suggest that he eat one of the people who came to greet him."

"You're right, Lazelan, she's wonderful." The big cat purred. "But is she really as adept as you say?"

"I'm convinced," Wolfbane stated, "Do you really want to find out?"

"No thank you," the male quickly replied as he looked around at the fighter, two guards, and now three mages.

"Scardy ca-" Wolfbane's teasing cut off in mid-sentence. The gnome wheeled around to silently confront Lazelan with his eyes. This was a trick that the mage had used before when the situation looked like the gnome's words were going to cause a fight. Lazelan ignored the smaller man's gestures and spoke to the queen instead.

"Why don't we go inside and we can catch up. If possible, we'd like to stay for a day or two before continuing on with our journey."

Sasha's nerves were shot. The knot in her core had tightened for a moment at what had almost happened. She could feel that the comfortable situation that they had created for themselves had been about to crumble. The gnome had sounded like he was egging the cat on for a fight, but Aylan was powerless to do anything should it have come to that. She wondered if Lazelan knew how close things had just come to disaster. At the suggestion that they go inside away from the sphinxes, she could feel the knot start to loosen.

As they started to turn for the door, Aylan called to the sphinxes. "Feel free to hunt or forage in the king's forest, but please abstain from eating any of my royal subjects." the queen invited. The giant cats began to flap their powerful wings, and lifted up into the sky. "Oh, and that includes the king's hunting party." She added as an extra security measure. "You might want to avoid that altogether!"

The knot tightened in the seer's stomach once more. The sphinxes had already started to fly off at the queen's offer, and Sasha didn't know if the giant cats had heard her warning.

Chapter 11
○ Such a Gem ○

For the first couple of seconds after the blacksmith of tigers-eye was turned up in Dain's hand, the other three honest dwarves just stayed frozen in their places in shock, though they were not really surprised.

It was not that they had expected Nalvo to cheat, far from it. The lack of honour used in this case was an affront to them all. Especially when the game was not just one of enjoyment, as they often played together. But when there was actually an important decision resting on the outcome, his dishonesty had put at risk the viability to continue using the card game to settle matters like these.

Dain tossed the card onto the table, where it landed in front of Nalvo as a silent accusation. Then he lowered his arms, allowing the green fur of his robe's cuffs to reach and warm his wrists once more. Not being an overly dramatic dwarf, but one of considerable girth, he sat.

The two older dwarves reacted first. Azagut's salt and pepper beard seemed to quiver as his mouth worked, trying to find the words to embody his disappointment without being overly crass. His face had begun to redden in his anger, and the purple trim that ran up the front of his robe and around the edge of the hood made the pallor of his skin look more severe as the fur brushed his neck and disappeared under his beard.

Durlak only grunted and sat like a stone in a mine cart. "Figures," he said grumpily.

Nalvo attempted to present them with his winningest smile, the one he used when he was about to use his charm to convince someone that what he wanted was what the other dwarf really wanted too. But looking around at the unforgiving faces of his peers, he let his smile fade. In fact, Odal thought that the other dwarf was beginning to look downright contrite. He also looked as if he wanted to raise the blue-rimmed hood attached to his cloak, and disappear into it, maybe indefinitely.

"You should go," Azagut finally managed in a low growl.

Defeated, and knowing that there was nothing that he could say to get himself out of his predicament, Nalvo stood and hooked his thumbs into the thick belt at his waist.

"Well, men, I'll leave you to it." he said almost congenially. Not one of the other dwarves bade him farewell.

"Not so fast," Dain stopped him in a quiet voice. The mage seemed ever so much more dangerous when he spoke with his voice lowered. It made the others always feel like he was going to evoke some monster to eliminate whatever was bothering him. The tone was sure, it said *I have already won*. Nalvo gulped, presumably in fright. It put a grin on Odal's face.

"I believe you owe Odal an apology," Dain pointed out. "Then you can go, and we'll deal with you later."

The part of Nalvo's face that could be seen amid his long blond hair and massive beard and mustaches paled visibly. Then that salesman's smile reappeared on his face. It was that same smile that said *you don't know me, but I'm your new best friend*.

"Oh, Odal knows that I didn't mean anything by it," he tried to convince the others.

"A right proper apology, cheater!" Azagut demanded, his Rs rolling regally with each word that contained them.

Nalvo's head tilted downward as his gaze dropped for a split second to the table and produced an exaggerated sigh of one burdened beyond what they can handle. Then he raised his blue eyes to Odal's brown ones, and said a simple, "I'm sorry, Odal."

To Odal, he sounded like a grumpy toddler who was only doing what he was told to appease a parent to get out of trouble. But he supposed that it was some consolation that at least he had said the words. Nalvo rarely apologized for anything he did, whether his wrongdoing was intentional or not. Odal decided to consider it a small victory.

"Gentlemen," Nalvo bid them farewell with the single word, and left them at the table. Once he had departed, the others sat contemplating what they would do about the yule feast.

"Now, everyone's welcome to his own opinion," Durlak began, but since Odal saved us all from being fooled by that little bit of treachery, I think he has more than earned the right to serve as host for the yule ball."

Odal felt a jolt of triumph and joy, followed by a sense of dread. There was going to be so much *work* to do. How had this happened? *A good deed never goes unpunished*, his father used to complain.

"It was really nothing, my friends," he said gruffly, "And I am honored by your suggestion, but I wouldn't want to rob Dain of the honor. After all, it was him that found the proof. Without that, my accusation would have been only my word against Nalvo's."

Although Dain was around the same age as Odal, he clapped Odal on the shoulder like a proud papa, and told him that he wouldn't dream of taking away such a grand honor for his trustworthy kinsman.

"You're a diamond in the rough, my friend." he added.

Odal found himself wishing that he had held his peace when he had noticed Nalvo cheating, but who knew, this could end up being fun. He had always been one to see the mine cart as half full, as opposed to half empty. Perhaps even Yili would come.

Azagut began to shuffle and deal the cards again, this time for a game just for fun. They were well into their third round when the warning calls came and the mountain began to rumble around them.

)

Chapter 12
◯ Suspension of Disbelief ◯

For the next two days, Sasha had felt almost normal again. Lazelan was back, and that meant that he and Aylan had resumed their work together, sharing the things they had learned while Lazelan had been gone. As a result, she found herself spending more time in Aylan's workroom like back in the days when the queen had still been learning about magic. The three of them were inseparable, although now they had a tag along.

"Don't touch that!" Lazelan warned as Wolfbane once again began to unstop one of the bottles on the shelf.

Sasha had at first been confused by why the mages had decided to divulge the location of their secret laboratory to this small stranger. But with Harmonium electing to avoid staying in the castle in lieu of visiting some of the more common inns and taverns, there was no one to keep the gnome out of trouble. And trouble found him like a pig found mud.

Sasha supposed that he wasn't a bad fellow by any means, but they had only been here for a few minutes, and he had already been warned about the dangers of the substances in the room fifteen times. The poor gnome was bored, and needed some recreation to keep him out of trouble. Come to think of it, his personality was very much like that of a puppy. But the queen had kept him close, because apparently the baby liked the sound of his voice. The more he talked, the less the baby kicked Aylan. The one time the gnome had ventured out into the marketplace to see what Endalwynndale had to offer, Aylan had had no peace from the baby until Wolfbane had returned to tell of what he had found.

Sasha saw the foreign script on the top page as Lazelan handed over the sheaves of paper that Xinnavane had given him. They were a new set of the old spells from the Almatraek Bright that he was on a quest to find. But it was only part of what they sought. No one knew where the Almatraek Bright or the Almatraek Dim had been hidden. They had both been spirited away and concealed by different groups of mages in the hopes of preserving the valuable spells within. They were a mixture of magic and herbology, and the information had come from more than one source. Each mage that had looked after the book had added a few of their best spells.

Sasha remembered the stories Lazelan had told Aylan about the twin set of books. The Almatraek Dim was full of attack spells, dark magic, created by power-hungry mages that didn't care who they hurt to achieve their desires. In contrast, the Almatraek Bright contained some of the only effective counter spells and antidotes for the evil in its sister book.

Endalwynndale had more than once been under attack from spells in the Almatraek Dim. When Aylan had defeated the mages who had come with the book to take over their kingdom, she had put the book under lock and key. Sasha knew that they had tried to destroy it, and she knew how frustrated the queen had become over not being able to. Now they were all hoping that if they found the Almatraek Bright, it might shed some light on the subject of how to successfully do it.

"Oof!" Aylan's hand flew to the side of her belly as the baby kicked or hit her from the inside.

"Wolfbane, would you tell the baby another story?" the queen asked.

Happy to have something to do, the gnome came to the table where Sasha and the mages were sitting, and hopped up on the last empty stool. He began telling the tale of their journey through the pyramid. Sasha became enwrapped in the tale as Lazelan continued to work with the queen to try to set her magic straight.

"Try something easy this time," Lazelan encouraged Aylan quietly over the cadences of the gnome's voice. "Just use a simple levitate spell to put the papers up on the shelf."

The queen raised her hand toward the pile of parchment, and said "Fli," *Levitate*.

For Sasha, the whole process was hard to observe. Over the years, she had watched her friend become better and better at magic. She had become powerful indeed, to the point where she could cast any spell without a spoken word or gesture. It was impressive to watch the queen sit as still as a statue, and to have all of the torches in the throne room alight at once when the king and queen were holding court and the sky began to dim at night time. Watching the queen's ability crumble and to see her having to go back to her elementary teachings, made Sasha feel pity for Aylan. It was like watching someone that had been injured in an accident try to relearn how to walk.

Sasha watched the papers sit on the table, as if no force was acting against them. But her attention was quickly drawn away as Wolfbane cried out.

"Hey!" he exclaimed as he began to lift off his seat. He frantically grabbed for the stool he was sitting on, trying to hold himself down to it. Instead, the stool began to rise with him as he held on. Aylan must have released the spell because the stool quickly returned to the floor with a thump, with the gnome still sitting on top of it.

"Ouch!" Aylan complained as her hand covered the spot where the babe had just kicked her. "Wolfbane, keep talking!" she advised. The gnome looked at her disbelievingly.

"I was just flying, and all you can think about is a story?" he asked.

"No, but the baby seems to like your voice." she replied.

Sasha found herself agreeing with the infant. One thing that could be said for the short fellow was that his voice had a warm soothing quality to it. It was no surprise that the baby might find it comforting, Sasha thought that she did too. Then the realization hit her like a ton of bricks. "It's the baby," she told them, "that's what is interfering with your magic.

"But it's not even born yet," Aylan objected, tenderly patting the side of her bulging belly. "Are you causing trouble in there?" she asked it, in a cutesy voice that Sasha had never heard the queen use before. It was the type of cadence that Sasha associated with the way small children would speak when talking to a puppy. Apparently Aylan got no kick as a reply, since she went back to trying to lift the papers once again with her magic.

"I'm not even sure that it's possible," Lazelan commented, but he looked deep in thought.

"I think that she might be right," Wolfbane agreed with Sasha.

They looked to the gnome as he spoke, only to find him hovering a few inches above his stool, with his arms crossed grumpily over his chest.

The queen gasped and looked to Lazelan, who shook his head to say that he wasn't the culprit. Instead, he tried to reassure her.

"It's okay, just release your spell." he said gingerly. But Aylan didn't reply to him. Instead, she spoke to the hovering gnome and Sasha felt a chill at the queen's next words.

"Be careful, Wolfbane, I'm not casting anymore."

)

Chapter 13
O Mount Up O

The deck of cards and the discard pile on the table shook until they toppled, fanning out the gems across the wooden tabletop.

Odal could feel the deep rumbling vibrations from the mountain travelling up the legs of his chair and into his legs and back. There were only two things that ever made the steadfast mountain shake like this, and he desperately hoped that it wasn't a cave-in.

Their mugs of stout ale rattled on the table as it shook, forming ripples that scurried across the foamy heads.

Cries of "Avalanche!" rang through the air. Odal felt some of the tension leave him although this was still somewhat of an emergency.

The dwarves possessed a certain amount of pride when it came to mining, after all, they had done it for generations going back thousands of years. It wasn't all they knew, but there was no doubt that it was what they knew best. Therefore, cave-ins, flooding of mineshafts, and explosions didn't happen often, but when they did, it was both embarrassing and deadly.

Still, an avalanche could be just as deadly if it had been a person that had set it off.

Durlak scooped up the cards with a sigh and shoved them back into the box.

"I suppose that's our cue to go," he yelled in a tired voice over the din.

"It must be another traveller." Azagut commented. He was probably right, no mountain dwarves would be the cause of one. They knew where to travel, what areas were most likely to be safe to traverse, and avoided planes of rock face that could build up the perfect sheet avalanche. Most travellers, especially ones that lived far from the mountains, wouldn't have the knowledge to avoid such places. It was amazing how many folks had made it to the city doors and had survived, simply because they hadn't weighed enough to cause the snow to slide.

Odal and his three companions stood, drained their mugs, and without pausing longer to push in their chairs, moved quickly to the closest of the three great doorways that allowed access to the mountain cities. In the large cavern before the large wooden doors, stood a set of cubbies containing extra outdoor clothing that the group of rescuers kept here for situations like these. In an emergency, they didn't want to have to travel through the dimly lit caverns to their own homes to get more outdoor wear, so here the things sat just in case they were ever needed. Thankfully, they weren't put to use that often. When the dwarves arrived, Nalvo was there with his hood up, already wrapping a scarf around his neck.

Living in the mountain meant that it was generally colder than whatever the climate was outside. As such, the normal attire for anyone in the dwarven clans consisted of layers of woolen robes like long-sleeved tunics, and then long coats made of thick animal hide or cured leather. One side of the hide on the front would wrap over the other like a house coat, creating a double thick layer across the torso, before being secured by a six to ten inch wide, heavy belt or colourful sash.

The garments were incredibly comfortable, and gave the dwarves' arms the full range of movement they would need to swing a pick in the mine or an axe in battle. The only down side was that the coats came down to their boots, enveloping their legs as they moved. It was fine for walking, but would make it difficult to climb or kick. Luckily, these were not activities that the mountain dwarves normally partook in.

The coats were usually all dark colours, save for the trim of coloured fur to help each other identify their clan. The animals that the pelts usually came from had adapted to be camouflaged out there amid trees and rock and stream, and it was useful to help the dwarves to blend into the rocky forest if they went venturing on the outside of Mount Embalk. Wearing the brown, black or grey garments also made it easier to spot each other in the event of an avalanche rescue, like the one they were about to attempt.

The one exception to the rule was always Nalvo, whose coat was made of white. He had gone down to the base of the mountain, and had stalked two white caribou for three days to get their pelts. Odal was glad that the other dwarf had chosen a darker coloured scarf to wrap around his neck for colour today. At least he had that much sense. It wouldn't do to go out to search for someone else, and then lose one of their own in the process. *Although, it is only Nalvo.* Odal quickly shook his head to clear it of the unpleasant thought. He wasn't a mean dwarf usually, he saw himself as one of the good guys. He was probably just still upset about winning the card game.

"I don't see why we have to keep rescuing these sun soakers," Nalvo complained as he strapped a pair of snowshoes to his large soft black boots.

"You wanted to be on the committee," Azagut reminded him. "Besides, maybe we'll get lucky and it will be *he who lights the way.*" he teased.

Odal chuckled, that wasn't exactly it, but it was a good one. In this area of Endalwynndale, there was a general knowledge of an ancient prophecy about a man that would come, some sort of great leader. The Carriers of Brightness called him *he who brightens the way*, and he was supposed to bring his followers to salvation. Most dwarves didn't put much stock in the teachings of the Carriers of Brightness, after all, it sounded like a religion designed for sun soakers. But once again, Nalvo differed from most, and he believed wholeheartedly that one day the man would come. Maybe not in their generation, but someday.

"I don't think so," Dain argued, "one would think that if he is supposed to be the saviour, then he would be able to save himself. I highly doubt that he'd need to be rescued if and when he does come."

Odal grunted, that made a certain amount of sense, if he were to pretend for a moment that the prophecy was even true. If it was, it would mean much more than a bunch of people joining the Carriers in their beliefs. It would also signify that there were other forces at work out there that the majority of folks, at least all of the ones Odal knew, understood to be child's tales. Seers would have to really exist for one thing, otherwise the prophecy could never have been written. Leave it to the sun soakers to come up with an idea like a person that could actually tell what the future would hold. The whole thing was just creepy. He decided that he'd leave religion to Nalvo.

He finished fastening the last buckle of his snowshoes around his sturdy boots, and donned the long toque that lay down his back. Odal loved his hat. His mother had crocheted it for him out of the three colours of their clan's gemstone, brown, gold, and orange, when he had gotten elected as clan chief. Most of the dwarves that had any business going outside had one in this style, because if the temperature dropped, the pointy end could be brought around in front of the throat and tucked up into the brim of the hat on the other side. It was like creating a sort of scarf or face covering, without having to have the extra garment with you that you couldn't really remove if you got hot with all of the hiking around.

Over the brim of his hat, Odal fastened the strap on a pair of goggles made of polished gems. The emeralds had been cut thinly, and had been polished to be as smooth as glass. They all wore a pair of these to protect the eyes from the onslaught of sun's rays once they got on the outside. Lastly, he stood, and pulled on his black fur-lined mittens.

"Whoever it is out there, I'm sure they're cold and in shock." Dain added, "So let's go."

The dwarves strapped shovels, a pick, a lantern, and a rope to their back as they waited for the rumbling to become still. For the first few seconds after an episode like this, it was always eerily quiet, like the silent mineshafts after the workers had all gone home.

They signaled the guards to open the tall doors, and each of the dwarves raised an arm to shield their eyes from the strong wind and the bright sun. Even though the day was overcast, it was a flood of natural light that the dwarves were not used to having to endure. The light made Odal's eyes hurt, and he half closed his lids for some respite.

"Let's get this over with as quickly as possible" He told the others. As they stepped out into the cold mountain air, they lowered their goggles and scanned the area to find out where the avalanche had occurred. With this weather, it was likely caused by wind-loading before someone walked on a weakened slab. With the almost non-stop fierce gusts hitting the dwarves though, they were fairly certain that they would have to cross the peak to the leeward side of the mountain to find their victim, and they would have to do so quickly.

Whoever was entombed in the snow, and there may be a whole group of journeymen that had shared the same fate, would only have about fifteen minutes of clean air before having to succumb to their demise.

Nalvo hastily pulled off one glove, and making an O shape with his first finger and thumb, placed them between his lips to whistle loudly. It was the whistle of a man trying to get someone's attention, and it worked.

Odal heard the distant cry of an eagle, and seconds later, a *whoosh* of air and a second cry of greeting as the majestic griffin descended from above. It had the head, feathery shoulders, and front talons of an eagle, while its sleek body, large rear paws, and tail were those of a lion. Odal thought that it looked magnificent and always found himself to be in a state of awe whenever the creature was around. As it came within forty feet of the party, each of the dwarves took a step back to give the creature the space it needed to land safely.

Nalvo spent a good deal of time outside the halls of sapphire that should have held most of his interest. But Odal had never seen the dwarf raise an axe in the mines. If one were to shake Nalvo's hand, they would find no respectable callouses made from years of hard work there. Instead, they would feel a smooth palm akin to the hands of one of the sun soaker lords. In truth, he was a very cunning ranger, and had the ability to become companions with everything from a burrowing mole to this sun-touched stately animal. He often headed the hunting parties that provided their communities with meat, and Odal would bet anything that he'd be gone for a few days before yule to lead another one.

As Nalvo began to climb onto the griffin's back, Odal could see that the ranger's white coat blended in with the animal's white head and wings. Perhaps the dwarf was not as much of a fool as Odal had thought.

The white clad dwarf murmured a few strange sounds to the creature. It turned its sharp hooked beak toward Odal and cocked its head to the side. Odal didn't know why, but he felt almost as if he were under its scrutiny. He shuffled his feet uncomfortably, and then did the only thing that felt right. He nodded his head with a slight bow in its direction, and talked to the great beast.

"Um, h-hello?" Odal stammered, unsure if the thing could even understand him. He decided to err on the side of caution, and consider that it might be able to. "Why, you are a beauteous and fine creature." he complimented it.

The animal screeched once before seeming to lose interest in the dwarf. Odal was relieved that it had, that thing looked as if it could bite a man's head off if it had a mind to.

"Come on Odal," Nalvo said congenially, "she consented to carry you too."

Odal's jaw dropped. "You want me to what?" he asked.

"Climb aboard, call it a gift, to make up for before." Nalvo beseeched.

Odal wasn't sure how scaring the pants off of him should be considered a gift, nor how it should make up for being accused of being a cheater. Even though he knew that precious seconds were ticking by, he continued to hesitate for a couple more.

"Um, actually, I'd rather-" Odal's attempt to back out of the situation was cut off by Nalvo waving his arms and emphatically shaking his head *no*, as if to ward him off. "Um, that is to say that I'd rather nothing else in this world." Odal finished with another bow. The eagle's eye fixed him in its gimlet gaze once more, and it screeched impatiently this time. That got Odal moving, and he gingerly threw a leg over the lion half of its back. It was warm to sit on, a pleasant contrast to the biting cold of the wind. Perhaps he would enjoy this, as long as he managed to keep his head.

"Now for the rest of us," Dain said, turning to face the huge arcing red doors that marked the entranceway to the cave. To either side of the tree-thick wooden doors sat a pair of gargoyles that looked as if they were carved from the mountain itself. Each stooped in its own recess that had been hewn from the side of the mountain; two just under the height of the handles on the door, and the other two above them closer to the top. The group always remained stone still, sitting at the ready for anything that would trigger their ability to move. They were the perfect unassuming sentries.

"We need a lift, please." Dain explained to the gargoyles. "I am sure you four heard the avalanche, and we only have minutes to save whoever is in peril."

A light dusting of snow had gathered on the flatter planes of the grey stone creatures; on their heads, the tops of their wings, their shoulders, and even their rounded knees as they crouched in their rocky slots. Each little patch of snowflakes fell off and blew to the ground as the grotesques began to move. Dain instructed them to follow the griffin as it leaped into the air. Three of the gargoyles unfurled their bat-like wings and took to the sky, grabbing

Dain, Azagut, and Durlak by the shoulders with their taloned feet as they went.

)

Chapter 14
O Heartless O

Oslan wheeled his horse around to pursue the elk that had changed direction again. The king's hunting party, made up of some of his knights, and a lord that had recently proven himself useful, followed suit. Their hoof beats were the sound of dulled thunder impacting the earth as the horses galloped after the large bull. This whole thing had turned into a mess. It was the reason that Oslan hated to go hunting with the nobles of his realm.

Normally Oslan relished the hunting trips with his closest friends. His most trusted knight, Carn, and three of the archers he had trained with as a boy, Bowregard, Thornton and Trembleton, were always willing to help him get a boar, elk, or even just a brace of rabbits for a meal. Truthfully, they used the time to unwind and allow themselves a small window of time to be the immature boys they still were at heart. Well, all except for Carn, maybe. Oslan was half convinced that the man had been born with all the seriousness of a grown up.

Because they had gone out so often together over the years, they had become a truly well-oiled hunting machine. Each one brought an important skill to the venture. Although Trembleton was a rather large fellow around the gut, he was a master on a horse, making his steed move as if he were as light as a feather. There had never been an obstacle that his horse couldn't jump. Bow was silent when he moved on foot, allowing him to sneak up on their prey. The closer you got, the harder it was to miss. Carn was an amazing tracker, and although Oslan wasn't bad himself, his knight saw evidence of the animal they hunted that even Oslan would have missed. Thorn was their long shot. If they ran into terrain that they couldn't easily traverse, like a boggy section of forest, he could make those long shots with an accuracy that was almost unfathomable. They worked well together, they had a tried, tested, and true system that usually worked, and they were familiar with each other's moves. They even had a set of hand signals worked out so that they could communicate with each other without spooking their quarry with the deep cadences of their voices.

Oslan hated to introduce a new unknown into the group. It was why any adult in their right mind would never hand a sharpened sword to a child just to see what would happen. Anyone with any kind of intelligence would know that it wouldn't end well for anyone involved. Much like today.

Oslan didn't doubt that Sir Stanton Sprig was a successful hunter most of the time. However the two squires that he had brought along, the older one was called Ruben, and the younger, Cal, were just so green. They had helped the king and queen to thwart the plot of a scheming herbologist that had tried to rise above his station dishonestly, and so they had been invited along for the expedition in case they could be of further service.

Two days ago, a pigeon had arrived with a frantic note from a ship sailing away from Ethic across the ocean. Two giant flying beasts had been spotted alighting on one of the islands, and the crew had been set to work to try to outrun the things while they presumably slept. The men had worked tirelessly, and the herbologist on board had been wise enough to send a message to both kingdoms, Ethik and Endalwynndale, to warn them of a possible attack.

In Aylan's condition, Oslan hadn't wanted to concern her or cause her any unnecessary stress without knowing exactly what was going on. So he told her that he was going to go hunting, took his most trusted knights with him, and led his party eastward toward the port town of Elbon. They found the town slightly disheveled, as if a celebration of happy news had occurred. When Oslan had inquired about it, he was told that the beasts had come, and that they were no threat. They had been carrying the kingdom's old mage, who was returning to Endalwynndale after a long stint away. They had marvelled at the animals, and told Oslan that they had just left that morning.

Oslan sent a pigeon after it to let Ormond know that there was no emergency after all, no siege or attack coming, but he supposed the chips would have to fall where they would. He knew full well that the giant cats would be able to outpace the pigeons easily. All he could do was try. But this left him with another problem. Although he wanted to get back to welcome his old friend, he had told Aylan that he had gone hunting. That meant that he had to return with some meat, which brought him to this unhappy task at hand.

Sprig's two squires were both so new to the sport of hunting, or perhaps they were just too nervous around the king, that they were making rookie mistakes. To make matters worse, it was almost as if they were trying to outdo each other to make their knight proud, but were bungling the whole trip in the process. Oslan was vexed at how long it had taken them to track down the elk, as the loud bickering of the boys and the fact that they often trod on the tracks that the king was trying to follow had slowed them so.

It had gotten to the point that although Oslan enjoyed having some time to himself with his companions, he sorely wished that Aylan had been there to put some kind of spell on them to make them as quiet and still as a crocodile. Oslan was starting to have serious doubts about wanting to have a child of his own, but he supposed it wouldn't be so bad with just one. There would be no one for it to argue with.

Sprig was clearly embarrassed by his squires' behaviour, and had finally ordered that they remain at the back of the group, and stay silent, lest they be sent back to the castle. They had glumly complied, and Carn had been able to find the elk's tracks again. The group had successfully snuck up on the beast as it stooped to drink from a deep section of river, and had managed to get within range of an arrow.

Thornton drew his father's bow to take careful aim. The king always insisted on a clean shot if possible. None of them wanted to see such a noble creature suffer from an ill placed arrow.

A poor shot could injure the animal, causing a wound that would still allow it to run off into the woods, possibly for miles before it finally became too pained or weak from loss of blood to go on. Scenarios like that were downright cruel to the animal, and more work for the hunters. However, the king had even seen disgusting lords that had thought themselves so superior that they had hurt an animal and not cared that it had run off to die somewhere. Those that were too lazy to bother finding it again were just despicable in Oslan's opinion. There were poor families within the kingdom who couldn't afford meat, and to let the animal die from the injury would mean that no one would benefit from the hunt. It was wasteful. The odd time that it had happened, the king had threatened to charge the unhappy lord for the loss of the meat unless they followed through with their kill, and they had not been welcomed back to the palace again.

Thornton was amazing though, Oslan had never seen him miss an animal's heart. Although almost a head shorter than the other two archers, he always handled his father's bow as if it had been made for him. Oslan knew that his friend had the elk in his sights, but as Thorn blew out the final steadying breath before his arrow's release, the two squires clamoured to be the one to shoot in order to down the animal first. Each nocked an arrow and had hurriedly taken aim, but while Cal drew back with his right hand, and Ruben pulled with his left, they jostled each other with their elbows. All three arrows were loosed, the two boys' haphazard shots a second before Thorn's sure one.

Both of the boy's shots went high. One flew right between the branches of the elk's left antler, and the other hit the right, glancing off it and causing the startled animal to bolt. As it leapt forward, Thorn's arrow, which would have been a clean shot to the heart, caught the elk in the ribs instead. Off it ran, and the hunting party tailed it in hot pursuit. The chase didn't last long. The injured elk got maybe as far as twice the length of their practice arena back at the castle before it fell.

The king called a halt to the horses to give the elk some space to take its last dying breaths. When it grew still, He instructed the two boys to pull out their hunting daggers.

"Have you boys ever quartered an elk before?" Oslan asked impatiently. He was trying to hold back his anger.

"I have, Your Majesty," Ruben said proudly as Cal shook his head no, looking a little green.

"Well today, you'll show him how to do it. Start with the throat." He ordered Ruben.

He asked Bow to watch over the lord and his squires, saying that he wanted to cool down by the river. Carn immediately started after him, but the king waved him away. After all, he was armed, and besides, what could possibly happen to him in the middle of the forest?

)

Chapter 15
O Snow Man O

They reached the peak within seconds. Of course, Odal didn't notice until he felt the griffin's soaring level out. Until then, he had been preoccupied with the feeling that he was going to fall off the back of the beast in a vertical drop as it climbed into the air. Once the flight evened out, he squinted through one eye that had been squeezed shut out of terror. Noticing the view of the mountain range and the way it scooped down to the valley below, he almost forgot his fright and opened his eyes. He also relinquished the death grip that he had put around Nalvo's middle, and sat a little straighter.

The other dwarf never chuckled or made fun of his fear. Odal would have to remember to thank him, provided he lived through the landing. While his eyes had been shut, Odal had been counting. It had taken his mind off of what he considered to be a near death experience, and he knew that in an avalanche rescue, it was important to keep track of how long the victim had potentially been caught in the snow. It could tell them what to expect when they found the person or people involved. Anything longer than fifteen minutes, and they would be running the risk of finding only corpses. They had seven minutes left to find the traveller and to dig them out no matter how far under they were.

"There!" Azagut called, pointing to a section of piled snow with something small and bright red laying on it.

Odal looked to the spot that his friend was pointing at. The crimson scarf stood out on the stark white snow like a ruby on a bed of quartz. He looked at the area around it, and saw no other signs of life. He wondered how many others were travelling with the person who was down there, and knew that they likely wouldn't be reached in time. The dwarves would have to start digging where their only point of reference was, and if they found the journeyman alive and conscious, they might be able to tell the dwarves who else they needed to search for.

As the gargoyles began to descend, Odal felt Nalvo lean back toward him until he almost ended up on Odal's lap. He was about to complain and tell Nalvo to get off him when the griffin tipped into a steep downward dive. Odal didn't have to worry about letting out a cry of fear, since it felt like his stomach had leaped up into his throat and was holding back the scream for him. He gritted his teeth against the feeling of his ale trying to come back up, and once again squeezed his eyes shut so as not to get vertigo as the ground raced toward them.

When the griffin touched down, Odal dismounted on shaky legs and kissed the frigid snow. He didn't care about how cold it was, it was currently his favourite thing in the world because it didn't move. Dwarves generally hated to ride even horses that were relatively close to the ground. But the griffin had made Odal much taller than a dwarf had any business being. *How did Nalvo do that? How could he like going up there? With that view of everything for miles around, why, you practically had warning about anything you might fall on.* Up there in the sky, that had been downright terrifying for Odal. Scary, and more than a little bit too exhilarating. He decided that he might have to get Nalvo to take him again, just to make sure that he hated it.

Odal rushed over to the scarf and gave it a tug to see if it had come free of the traveller. It stuck fast in the snow, and appeared to be going straight

Foresight's Flight

down. He began to dig with his hands as Nalvo unstrapped his shovel.

The gargoyles dropped off their passengers and they joined Odal and Nalvo, who had already gotten down a foot deep. The scarf kept going, and so would they. Durlak began to yell down into the snow to let the victim know that the dwarves were there, and that the travellers would soon be safe.

Mentally, Odal was still counting down the minutes in his head, and he was getting nervous as time was running out. It was always easier to rescue someone that was conscious, because they would start calling for help and you would know when you were close so you could avoid hitting them with the shovel. However the rescuers had to move slower when there was no warning, just so they didn't accidently kill the journeyman with their rescue gear.

Down the dwarves tunneled until the shovels rang out with a metallic clang. Confused, Odal threw his spade aside and felt with his hands. Looking at the snow, there didn't seem to be anything there to stop the shovels, but feeling with his mittens, there was something hard holding up the snow. If Odal didn't know any better, he would have sworn that it was a pane of glass. But the dwarves knew this mountain like the back of their hands, and no structures had ever stood in this place.

Odal used his hands to wipe the snow off of the surface, and saw that the scarf had penetrated the substance and the other end dangled limply from it on the inside. The sight that shocked Odal though was under the scarf. There, in the middle of a large flattened circle of snow, was a man in strange attire that sat cross-legged on a small carpet eating a pastry of some sort.

Chapter 16
O Eye Spy O

As Oslan walked away to cool his emotions, he heard the wet sounds of the older of Sprig's squires cutting through the hide, followed by the gagging splatter of the younger squire sicking-up onto the forest floor. Oslan grimaced and didn't bother turning or stopping. He wanted to outdistance the stench of stomach bile before it got to him. This happened to lots of boys on their first hunt. It happened to many men at their first battle too. Oslan supposed that when the situation was intense, or more violent or gory than what they were expecting to have to handle, sometimes the mind and body just became overwhelmed.

"Away from the meat!" He heard Sprig order the boy as he got ill.

"What about me?" Ruben demanded incredulously.

"Yes, away from Ruben too, of course," Sprig said hastily, then added "Ruben, you had better step away from the meat too, I think he might have gotten some on you. Go wash it off and come back to finish your task."

"Ug!" Ruben uttered in disgust.

Despite his peevish mood, Oslan chuckled under his breath. *I'm glad that had never happened to me. Then again, my father began taking me hunting as soon as I had learned to sit a horse, practically as soon as I had begun to walk.* He began to feel melancholy, glad for what his father had taught him, and began to miss him. He knew that he had been lucky; not every boy had a father around to teach him things, especially if he had to travel for work, or was killed in battle or by disease. Oslan didn't know how Cal had gotten this far through life without having had this experience, but maybe it was a good thing. *Perhaps that is what the boys will need to make this a memorable enough experience that they can learn from it. There is hope yet.*

Oslan knelt by the thick stream and peered into the clear water. It was moving pretty quickly out in the middle where the current would take the water to the bay beside Elbon. But Oslan had found a shallower inlet, no deeper than twice his height, where the water moved at a slower pace. Looking at the span of water as a whole, Oslan could see the clouds reflected back toward the sky as if they were moving and alive with the water's rippling and churning surface. The sight was beautiful, and began to calm him.

He knelt on a wide flat rock that cut into the water steeply. The first foot or so that was submerged was growing a green layer of algae. He noted that an inch or two of the rock that stuck out of the water, appeared to be getting wet at intervals as the water lapped upon it, and also sported the green stuff. He would have to be careful not to tread on that that or he very well might slip and go in.

He concentrated on the solid reflection of his face and noted that it was looking a little pale, probably as a reaction to the retching sounds coming from the area where the bull lay. He brought his hands together and dipped them into the water, collecting it in his palms that were cupped like a bowl. He took a cool drink and let the rest trickle back in, each droplet refracting the light from the sun in a hundred shiny moving elongated spheres.

He heard a succession of deep earthy thumping footfalls growing closer and the quick breathing of a runner as Ruben jogged over to clean himself in the water beside him. *Can't you find another spot?* the king lamented. The squire was the last person he wanted to see right now. He just wanted to be left alone for the moment. Being the king, he so rarely got any time to himself to just think. To his surprise, it was almost as if the boy had heard his thoughts, because he picked a spot a little ways downstream from the king.

Oslan used his hands to once again scoop some water up, and this time, splashed his face with it to enliven himself. The water was cold and felt refreshing, melting away his anger.

Then Ruben hollered, "There's a girl in the stream! Help, men!"

Oslan quickly wiped the dripping water from his face and eyes. He saw Ruben starting to doff his breastplate. He would sink like a stone if he left it on and tried to go in after the girl. As it was though, it didn't look good. There was no splashing. Nor was there any flailing of a drowning victim. Oslan had seen no bobbing head coming up for air. As Ruben fiddled with the buckle, Carn and Sprig rushed over to him, scanning the water, and asking where he had seen her.

They searched the clear water, but could see no one, and Oslan turned to the pool where he knelt to see if the person had been spotted closer to him upstream, or being swept away in the current. He traced from where the current to the spot by his knees, and was startled. Before he could even register the golden eyes before him, he started in surprise as a pair of slender white arms reached up from the water, grabbed him around the back of the neck, and pulled him into the river.

)

Chapter 17
O Fall Guy O

As Odal stared down into the round space devoid of snow under him, The funny man ate the last bit of his pastry and carefully licked the tip of each finger that had been holding it.

Odal tried to clear a bigger hole in the snow, and it was only then that the man glanced up with a start, as if just noticing him. The stranger stood in a fluid motion and gave him a subdued smile. The tall bald figure had bronze coloured skin, and wore cream coloured pants that were gathered at the ankles with gold bands. For a top, he had some garment that only hinted at being a tunic. It was wide at the shoulders, with peaked epaulets of gold, but as it tapered downward, it wasn't quite as wide as his body so, that the sides were left open. It was made of a creamy material that matched his pants, and the tunic flowed to just above his ankles. A sash of gold that matched his pant cuffs was wrapped around and around the tunic at the top of the pants, rising in a thick band half-way up his torso. It was knotted at the side so that the golden tassels that hung down danced by the side of his leg as he moved. Odal would bet that the man was freezing, although, by his manner, that seemed not to be the case.

Then Odal saw the glint of inch-wide gold chain links and a pendant in the shape of a torch that hung over the sash that held the man's tunic in place.

If this man was who he appeared to be, then Nalvo was never going to let them hear the end of it.

The golden torch was the telltale symbol for the Carriers of Brightness, but what would one of their brothers be doing here? They were an organized community of mages that lived to share what they called *the prophesy*, and their other beliefs to anyone who wished to listen. They would go to small communities and perform miracle-like acts with their magic, telling the townsfolk that they were only paving the way for *he who brightens the way* to bring light to the masses.

Odal scrambled backwards as the Brother lifted an arm to focus his palm on the spot that the dwarf's face had occupied a moment before.

Silently, a crack in the invisible dome began to open, and it freed the scarf. As it fell toward the man, the carpet he was standing on began to ripple. Odal's mouth dropped open as the mat began to lift the man into the air. He warned the others to get back, and they started to inch their way back off of the snowy mound. The Brother easily caught the tumbling scarf, whereupon it turned into a thick gold chain bearing a heavy charm with yet another torch, which he placed around his neck.

The carpet rose upward until the man hovered with his head just under the cleared space on the glass-like barrier that held back the snow. Then the man snapped his fingers, and as if the glassy ball had popped like a bubble, the snow that the dwarves stood on began to cave in. The Carrier calmly emerged through the hole and stayed on his mat, presumably to watch the whole thing play out. The look on Nalvo's face at seeing the Carrier was that of a lost child being saved.

Fear gripped the rest of the dwarves, however, as the ground that had seemed so solid under them shifted and began to free fall from the area that Odal had cleared. They began to clamber as fast as they could away from that point as the snow plummeted down in a rolling ring that moved outward. The weight of the snow on the upper side of the mountain bore down on the space, sliding again in another mini avalanche to fill the gap now that nothing held it back.

Heavy mountain dwarves did not move fast as a general rule, and every member of the rescue party wore snow shoes, which slowed their gait even more. Odal felt like he was trying to run in a dream, where all he could manage was a slow motion sort of progress. The falling ring of snow was growing nearer and nearer to where he struggled. The other dwarves had kept themselves back from the window-like pane that Odal had found, and they were starting to make good headway to safety. But Odal had been only a few steps from the hole, making him the closest to disaster. He took the wide steps of a person wearing snowshoes, and yelled at Nalvo to run. The ring chased him, the snow falling faster than Odal could move, until he finally reached the spot where Nalvo was still just standing in awe. Odal grabbed Nalvo's arm and tried to drag the other dwarf with him when the moving snow fell away from under them both.

Odal didn't have time to comprehend the look of disbelief and betrayal on Nalvo's face. It was the face of a man whose core understandings that had been held his whole life, had just been shattered. Odal was oblivious. He held onto Nalvo's arm as best he could as they fell and then landed in the newly exposed snowy crater, packed down by the man's invisible sphere. He had no chance to move before the moving heavy snow slammed into them and then continuing to pile up around and then over them.

All he was aware of now was the scream coming from his throat and the darkening snow piling up around him. It came to a stop quickly, the dull thuds of more clods of snow hitting the pile began to peter out.

He felt the snow pressing in on him. The blanket of frigid white was so heavy that he had lost the ability to move. He sat suspended in the dark snow, being squeezed on all sides and from every angle. He wasn't even sure if Nalvo's arm was still in his grasp or not. Anywhere that the snow touched his flesh; on his neck between his collar and hat, on his cheeks and nose, the annoying space on his wrist between his jacket and his warm mitten, the snow touched his flesh and began to burn him with cold. At all of these spots, wet drops of melting snow tried to trickle into his collar and down his back, or up his sleeves. The snow held against his cheeks and nose were beginning to make his skin hurt.

He began counting, slow and steady, ticking away the seconds of the quarter of an hour that he had left to live.

○

Chapter 19
O A Quick Getaway O

Wolfbane continued to hover over the stool, frantic to be let down. Aylan had tried to stop the spell, but she wasn't the one controlling it. You couldn't force someone else to stop casting. The only time a mage was usually cut off from his or her magic ability was when she was asleep, drained, or dead. But Sasha remembered that Aylan had already proven that the former wasn't always the case, as she had actually cast her first spell during the heart of a nightmare.

The four were trying to come up with ideas of how to get the gnome down without hurting the queen or her child, but so far each idea had come up short.

"We need to find the Almatraek Bright!" Lazelan fumed. As their ideas had run out, he had begun to pace quickly back and forth in the small room. "If we're lucky, an answer may lay within its pages. Other mages before you have had to have been with child! There must be some notes about it in the book."

Aylan opened her mouth to respond, but remained silent. She seemed to swoon as the spell continued to make Wolfbane float, and she grabbed the table for support. Lazelan caught her and tried to steady her on her feet.

"I'm getting weak, Lazelan, we have to do something! What if the baby uses up the last of my energy? I can't lose the ability to cast forever. Please, think!" She pleaded with them all.

Sasha tried to come up with something, but her experience with magic was limited to what she had seen Aylan or Lazelan do. She had witnessed lots of townspeople come to ask Aylan for herbology potions and lotions for various ailments from cuts to colds to insomnia. She felt like there could be something to that, she just had to figure out what it was. Then it came to her like a spark in the dark, and she had it.

"What about a sleeping draught?" Sasha asked. If you drink enough of it, the baby will surely get some too. Maybe if we can make it fall asleep, the spell will end."

"It's worth a try." Lazelan decided. He strode over to the glass potion bottles that sat neatly lined up on the shelves against the wall. He read over the labels written in Aylan's flowing script until he found one that she had called *sound slumber*. He handed the vial to the queen.

"This might work for now," Aylan warned them, "but we need to find a more reasonable solution. I can't spend the rest of my pregnancy unconscious; I have a country to run, especially with Oslan away."

Lazelan agreed with her, "Yes, of course. But for now, can you make it back to your room before you take this?" he asked doubtfully.

Sasha protested at once. "We can't get her back to her bed first; we don't know what will happen to Wolfbane. For all we know, he could end up floating down the hall after us! Or worse, the baby could end the spell when we're mid-way up the stairs." It was strange that this had been her first thought. Aylan was her best friend, and yet, her primary concern just then had been about the gnome. The mental image she had gotten of him being dropped on his head had made her cringe for some reason. She glanced at him and quickly looked away. It had not been long enough to be considered staring, but it had been sufficient for her to realize that he had a great head of hair, just plain brown, but with a slight wave to it.

Aylan looked as though she were fading fast.

"Drink it now," Lazelan ordered hastily, taking the little round bottle long enough to pull the stopper before folding it back into her hand. Sasha watched in trepidation as the queen drained the bottle. The seer had no idea how long the concoction would take to work, or how long it would last. She wondered if it were safe to wake someone under the potion's effects, in case of an emergency that needed her attention while Oslan was gone. She had so many questions, but before she could voice even one, Aylan's eyes rolled up into her head and slipped shut. As Wolfbane fell to the floor with a cry of surprise, the queen slumped into Lazelan's arms.

Now Sasha knew that the ginger-haired man was talented. After all, Lazelan had served Oslan's father as his mage for years before teaching Aylan herself. He was powerful and smart, however, he was also tall and lanky, and didn't have much upper body strength to speak of. In fact, he appeared to be floundering under the weight of the queen and the girth of her unborn child. There were only so many ways one could grab an unconscious person, and unfortunately for the queen, not many of them that Lazelan could manage were very dignified.

Finally, Lazelan decided on supporting the queen from behind, by hooking his arms under her armpits. Sasha rushed forward to try to lift the queen's feet off the ground. It was a struggle. Wolfbane rushed ahead to open the door before them, and Sasha backed up, straining under the weight herself. Dresses were definitely not designed to be worn during a bout of manual labour, and the floor-length skirt made it difficult to step backward down the hall without having the hem slip under her heels.

Wolfbane made as if he were going to support the queen from underneath in the middle, but Sasha stopped him before he laid his hands on the queen, pointing out that the queen would probably not appreciate having his wee hands planted on her posterior.

Instead, he tried to be helpful by lifting the back of Sasha's skirt off the ground whenever she trod on it. Each time, she pictured a roguish grin on his face as she imagined that he was probably getting an indecent flash of her shapely ankles. It might be true that she actually liked his sense of humour, and maybe she had noticed that he had a rather handsome visage, but still, she wasn't going to act like a strumpet for the man. Thankfully, he kept any comments about the situation to himself. She liked him for that.

They struggled down the narrow passageway and out into the empty war room, where Wolfbane pulled out a chair at the heavy wooden table to allow Sasha and Lazelan to set the queen down.

Quickly, Wolfbane unfurled one of the maps on the table and laid it in front of the queen. Then he instructed Lazelan to help him lean the queen forward, while he told Sasha to arrange Aylan's arms on the table so they crossed one another. As Lazelan brought her the rest of the way forward, the gnome told Sasha to place her head on her arms as if they were a pillow.

"You two sit as well, pretend to be in some deep discussion," he ordered as he walked out the door. Sasha could hear the rise and fall of his voice, and his amiable chuckle before the sound of his quick footfalls returned with a second person in tow. As the door to the war room opened, Wolfbane entered with one of the two guards that had been outside the armoury. Sasha pointed to the map.

"No, the only place it makes sense is here!" She told him emphatically. Wolfbane interrupted the false conversation with the one he was having with the guard.

"See, as I told you, the poor dear is right tuckered out listening to these two bicker," he said sweetly, as if explaining the queen's current condition to the guard. Sasha was taken aback at the suggestion that she had anything to do with it, and due to an immature quarrel like that of a child! But before she could say anything to the point, he went on.

"Truthfully, I think her royal highness is really just feeling the effects of her pregnancy. You know how these things go. I would suggest that you might take her up to her room without waking her. I would do it myself, but as I am still somewhat of a stranger here, I wouldn't deign to lay my hands upon the queen. But you, with such an important station as you were at, I'm sure that she would easily put her faith in you."

The guard immediately gave him a nod, and bent to easily lift the queen. He carried her the way a father would carry his little girl, with her head lulling against his shoulder. To Sasha, she seemed so small and fragile in his arms. Well, all except for her enormous belly.

Once they got to her room and Millie had allowed them in, the knight placed Aylan in her bed, and Millie pulled the covers over her to let her sleep.

As they left the queen's quarters, Wolfbane thanked the guard and dismissed him back to his post.

They left the handmaid with the queen, letting her know not to wake Aylan. Lazelan also asked Millie to let the queen know the very second that she woke, that she was not to try to cast anymore magic under any circumstances. They had no idea how the child had managed to hijack Aylan's spell, but he hoped against hope that perhaps it only had the power to maintain one, and hopefully not to create one of its own.

Lazelan decided that it would be better if they weren't there when the queen woke up to avoid this continuing to happen to the gnome. He sent a messenger to collect Harmonium Magster from the inn, and hoped that he would be quick in coming. But instead, the messenger came back alone to tell them that Harmonium had received a mysterious note the day before. Upon reading it, he had immediately fled, and hadn't been seen in the city since.

Lazelan looked truly vexed at the news, but they readied the Sphinxes for the next leg of their flight all the same. Sasha tried to comfort Lazelan by reminding him that Harmonium could take care of himself. Her friend nodded in agreement, but only looked slightly less worried despite her efforts. She knew that they had to go, time was wasting. She called for Sabyn and ordered a pack to be made for each of the travellers.

The minutes until the satchels were ready seemed to drag on, as they all made small talk of their hopes that the now slightly smaller party could make a clean getaway before the queen was to wake. Lazelan promised to do his best to find the Almatraek Bright, and return with it as soon as possible.

Lazelan squeezed her hand and said goodbye with a brotherly peck on her cheek. Then he climbed up to the sphinx's shoulders, and looked in the direction that they would be heading. Sasha knew her friend well, and she strongly suspected that he was still lost in thought about Harmonium's wordless disappearance.

She jumped as someone took her hand. There stood the waist-high gnome, with her fingers held lightly in his. His dark grey eyes looked up at her. They were made to almost glow with facets of gold running through them that reflected the sunlight. She found herself wondering if she had noticed that before.

"It has been a real privilege to have met you, Lady Sasha." he stated in a low voice for just the two of them to hear. Her name had come out as a hallowed whisper. In her stomach, an imaginary fish began to flop around, and she suddenly felt very warm all over. She liked the way her name had sounded coming off his tongue. She had to supress a young girl's giggle. *What is wrong with me?*

He could not bow and bend to kiss the back of her hand the way a true knight might have, as his stature wouldn't allow it. He raised her hand to his face instead, and as his gentle lips brushed against the back of her knuckles, she was flooded by a tingling that nearly undid her wits.

"The privilege has been all mine," Sasha told him. It was a perfectly normal response to the sentiment, however, for some reason it had come out quite breathlessly.

Just then, Sabyn arrived with four packs, and Wolfbane hastily let Sasha's hand go. For some strange reason, the withdrawing of his hand felt like a great loss of some kind. She busied herself by helping Sabyn hand out what she had brought from the kitchen.

The handmaid had arrived with two smaller packages for the travellers, and two rather large ones for the cats, who gave them a good sniff and began to purr. Wolfbane accepted his humbly and climbed aboard the sphinx that was waiting for him.

Sasha bade them farewell, and as the sphinxes took to the blue sky, she wished them luck and called out to them.

"May brightness be behind you all!"

She waited until they were only specs on the horizon, and realized that she wanted them to make their way back to the palace quickly on their return. She wondered if they would be safe, and unexpectedly, she found herself wishing that she would get the chance to see Wolfbane again.

With all the excitement for the day done, she returned to her room to put herself into a trance to try to see where their adventure would lead them. As she drifted off to a sleep very different than Aylan's, she remembered Lazelan's warning to Millie, and hoped that the girl would remember to deliver the message to the queen.

Chapter 20
O Something Fishy O

Oslan gasped as the slender arms pulled him off balance, making him plunge forward into the cold water of the river. He had gotten just enough air to fill a portion of his lungs. He wouldn't be able to stay under for long. He was so surprised that at first he didn't try to fight it. The girl had high cheek bones, and a dainty nose, but something was a bit off with her neck. It was like the skin there was pulsing in a succession of tiny flaps. Then he noticed that her shoulders were bare. *Is she naked?*

He averted his eyes back to her face out of respect. Her black hair floated in the water around her, almost dancing as she tried to speak. Those seaweed-green round eyes stared at him pleadingly. Her full red lips moved, but no intelligible words came out. It was like each bubble contained its own little syllable, and when she tried to speak they all got jumbled on their way up to the surface. He couldn't understand her, and his lungs were starting to burn with the need for more air.

A strong hand dove into the water to grab the king and began to pull him back out. The green eyes of the maiden in front of him widened with surprise, but it wasn't until he realized that the strange girl had no intentions of letting go, that he began to struggle. He had to get air, he needed her to let go, but she held him fast. A second hand, Carn's, he supposed, joined the first and heaved at the king.

Carn was a strong man, and Oslan's head actually broke the surface long enough to get another good breath of air. The men were yelling to each other, trying to save their king. He came out another few inches despite the weight of the girl clinging to him, but it seemed as if Carn was having difficulty holding him.

A long green fish tail that Oslan hadn't noticed before stroked powerfully in the river and drew him back into the water completely. As Carn temporarily lost his grip, and the king's head was dunked again, Oslan heard Bow exclaim "She's a mermaid!" before his ears were under.

Shocked, he looked down at where her legs should have been to confirm this, even risking the fact that she might be wearing no clothes. She was though, after a fashion. She wore a green top of sorts that had been expertly woven out of seaweed, and decorated with shells. It clung to her as she floated in the water, but it only covered her from under her arms to mid-way down her torso. He had never seen anything like it, and his cheeks flushed despite the coolness of the water around them. He supposed that it made a certain amount of sense, a girl couldn't rightly swim in a gown, but he was seeing parts of her that no man had the right to see on a strange woman. Her bare shoulder, the curve of her sides, her navel! Oslan went bright red and screwed his eyes shut, trying very hard to think of Aylan. He had never so much as peeked at the ankle of another woman before, and this was just, well, too much. He had seen it though. Out of the corner of his eye, he had caught the flicking of a long green scaly fish-like tail.

What does she want with me? He couldn't fathom what it might be. He knew that she was trying to tell him something, but what? He couldn't understand her under water, and he had no idea if mermaids could even go up on land. His lungs were desperate for air again. He had to think, he had to make her understand. He opened his eyes and trained them on her face, taking special care not to let them wander. He pointed to his mouth and let out an air bubble. He placed his hand flat on his chest and made his face into a pained expression. He reached up and ran his fingers over the flaps of skin on her neck. *Gills, they must be gills*, he told himself.

She shuddered and knocked his hand away, but nodded. The king let out some of his used up air. His lungs were afire now, screaming for more oxygen. The loss of some of his breath seemed to have relieved some of the pain, but he had to get to the surface, and he needed to go now. He began to kick off the bottom, and rose an inch before her skinny arms pulled him back to her. *How can she be so strong?* he couldn't fathom in his state of panic. He realized that she wasn't going to let him go up. Instead, she pulled him to her, placed her lips over his and began to blow life-saving air into his mouth.

The gills on her neck worked furiously, until she pulled away and coughed out bubbles twice. Her body wasn't made for breathing for two, Oslan guessed. Now when she held him, it seemed as if she was doing it more for support than to capture him. He let out some of the air while trying to ask if she was alright. She looked at him quizzically, apparently unable to understand him either.

Carn's hands re-appeared in the river, but this time he grabbed the girl. When the mermaid's eyes widened in terror and she let out a bubbling blood-curling scream, Oslan didn't need a translator to know that as the knight pulled her out of the water she knew that she was going to die. At the same time, two more pairs of hands grabbed the king and hauled him to safety up out of the water and onto the forest floor.

Oslan choked and sputtered, having taken in some water on the way out. His clothes clung heavily to him as the water drizzled off his doublet in rivulets. He impatiently pushed his thick brown hair off his forehead to stop his curling bangs from dribbling into his eyes, and looked to where the girl lay scrabbling by the edge of the stream.

She lay on her belly, hands clawing at her neck and the bank, writhing on the ground as if she were in pain. She was trying to pull herself back toward the river, but she could find no purchase, as the newly fallen leaves she lay on simply stuck to her wet skin and moved with the palms of her hands. She made a sickening sucking sound as she tried to breathe the water that was no longer around her. Rolling onto her back, she tried to find the king with her eyes. She pointed frantically at the water, beseeching him for mercy. The others just stood over her in shock.

Her voice was comprised of a strange gasping sound over reedy vocal chords that were not used to being used. It was almost as if she was trying to talk by sucking in the air past them, instead of blowing it out.

"Whaaaa-derrr." *water,* Oslan understood at once.

"If I point to the sky, come save me," he told the others. Then he lunged toward the mermaid, scooped her up, and leapt back into the water with her in his arms.

Chapter 21
O Down for the Count O

Odal was beginning to feel lightheaded. He was still counting, and several minutes had already gone by. He was starting to wonder what had happened to his friends. They had presumably seen where Nalvo and he had gone down. There shouldn't be any reason why it should be taking so long for the other dwarves to rescue them. But Odal was surrounded by silence. He hadn't heard the crunching of footsteps above, nor the talking of voices. Even Nalvo's bellowed curse words had stopped. Odal knew that Nalvo must be close to him, but the other dwarf was still out of reach.

At first Odal had tried to struggle, but now he understood that no amount of strength was going to allow him to move within his sarcophagus of tightly packed snow. The ice probably continued to melt on his cheeks and against the rest of his exposed skin, but now it was all just numb. The panic was even subsiding in his exhaustion. He wanted to fall asleep, but some nagging feeling in the back of his mind was letting him know that it wasn't a good idea. He had to keep counting.

It was dark. He couldn't see a thing. To tell the truth, he wasn't even sure if his eyes were opened or closed. Remembering seemed too difficult. He was rambling off a stream of numbers in his head, but he was beginning to forget why. He couldn't hear a thing. He was used to the vast caverns under the mountains, and the almost constant echoes that followed any movement or uttered word. Now there was only insulated silence. At first he had tried to call for help, but the snow seemed to swallow up the sound the second that it had left his mouth. He had stopped calling to be saved. He wanted to conserve oxygen. Yelling only filled the small pocket of air he had left with unbreathable used-up breath. He was so tired now, and a bit dizzy. It was becoming increasingly difficult to keep his thoughts in order. Maybe he'd just take a little nap. His repetitious counting slowed and stopped.

Consciousness came back to Odal in slow stages of awareness. As he climbed out of a dream, becoming more alert by the second, the first thing that he noticed was the lack of pressure on his body from the snow. He was lying down and his limbs were comfortably stretched out. He opened his eyes to find that he was inside the mountain. He was lying in a comfortable bed with heaps of blankets on top of him, making him start to sweat. Evidently, they had been trying to bring up his body temperature.

He threw off two of the top covers, and noticed the lavishly decorated room. It was evident that someone wealthy lived here. The room was large and had a plush arm chair in the corner, as well as a second empty bed beside the one that Odal was occupying. A wash stand and pitcher stood in the corner, as well as a writing desk with a second high-backed chair. A painting of a blond dwarven woman in an elegant gown, holding a bouquet of flowers hung on the wall opposite the beds. The elaborate gilt frame was almost half a foot wide. The place was gorgeous, but there was an odd underwater ambiance to the room that Odal wasn't familiar with. The shimmering walls were blue.

"Nalvo?" Odal asked, turning his head toward the door.

In walked his companion, wearing a flowing silky robe over warm pajamas. A second dwarf with blond hair entered behind him, carrying a tray with a steaming mug. This was Duerna, his wife. Odal could see the resemblance between her and the maid in the painting on the wall now. Perhaps it was a painting of her sister, or a matron from farther on down the line. Nalvo helped Odal to sit up, and Duerna placed the tray on Odal's lap. He wasn't sure what would be in the mug, but he was fairly sure that he had no appetite. Still, he lifted the steaming cup out of consideration for her. He thanked her and then turned to Nalvo, who had turned the chair away from the desk to face the bed.

"What happened?" Odal asked as he took his first sip. Hot tea almost scorched his gullet going down, but it also instantly soothed him from the inside out. He thanked Duerna, and she graced him with a smile before she left them alone. Nalvo sat in the chair and planted his hands on his knees, leaning forward as if to tell an amazing story.

"He is a visitor from an ancient land, a Carrier of Brightness! What are the chances of one actually coming here?" Nalvo was gushing like an excited young dwarf that had just mined his first gemstone.

"He almost killed us," Odal pointed out, not caring where the man was from.

"He *saved* us!" Nalvo contradicted. He had clearly already put the man on a pedestal just because of his vocation. Odal knew that he wasn't going to win this argument, but that had never stopped him from pointing out the obvious to a fool.

"Well he must not be the brightest torch on the wall; I stopped counting at around eleven minutes. For a mage, that's almost forever. We were practically dead. After seeing the way he had held back the avalanche, he probably could have just lifted the snow off of us and let us climb out." Odal insisted. Nalvo looked down at his hands. The man appeared to be embarrassed. "Nalvo, what aren't you telling me?" Odal asked, knowing that something was up.

"Well, heh heh," Nalvo laughed nervously. He very rarely got anxious. Pompous, over-bearing, and snooty, yes, but not usually unnerved. Something was up.

"Spit it out," Odal ordered flatly.

"Well, he actually rescued me mere seconds after we went down," Nalvo confessed. Odal was shocked. They must have been separated further apart than he had originally thought. He hadn't heard anything. Though it would explain why Nalvo had stopped calling for help so quickly. "I might have gone a bit overboard when I heard who he was. I just had so many questions. He told us about the prophecy. But what he really came for was to see Dain! Can you believe it?" Nalvo spouted in an almost non-stop rant. Odal was pretty certain that the dwarf hadn't even taken a breath in between sentences.

Odal looked into his mug. He drank down the steamy liquid. It soothed him and calmed him, which was good. So his ally had been rescued right away, and instead of letting the mage rescue his friend, Nalvo had decided to talk philosophy instead. Odal's blood boiled. *I might have died!* Odal was pretty sure that he almost had! He took another sip. It gave him a chance to reign in his anger, because he was almost ready to let his fists start doing the talking for him. He counted to ten to calm himself further, to the point where he could talk civilly to the *friend* who had almost let death take him. Then he asked Nalvo the only other thing that really mattered at this point.

"What does he want with Dain?"

Chapter 22
O Hide and Seek O

Oslan hugged the sopping slippery mermaid to him as they splashed into the frigid river. It wasn't very deep where he had jumped in, and his feet hit the bottom much more quickly than he had anticipated. His teeth clacked together painfully as he was jarred to a sudden stop. Then his arms were empty as the mermaid easily swam away from him with a single flick of her tail. Enveloped once more in the cocoon of water, the mermaid's ability to breathe seemed to have been restored.

"I'm sorry," he tried to tell her. The result was the same rolling bubbly type of speech as before. She looked at him with indecision on her face. He needed to come up with a way for them to communicate with each other. He wanted to know who she was, where she came from, and why she had almost drowned him.

He searched their surroundings for something that might help him. The bottom was mostly rock and sand with the odd sprig of grass=like seaweed growing toward the surface. A old branch that had long ago fallen from a tree was wedged under a boulder, but Oslan didn't think that it would be any help. Then he spotted the rocky ledge that he had been kneeling on when the girl had first pulled him into the water. From above, it had looked like almost a sheer drop straight down, but from underwater, he could see that it had been hiding a small alcove below it. Perhaps he could find a shell or a small pebble to write a message on the rocky wall. He swam under the rock shelf and to his surprise, he found a small cave with a pocket of air between the top of the water and a concave section of the stone above. He gratefully poked his head up out of the water and took a deep breath. He was about to dive back down the way he had come when the mermaid's face broke the surface beside his.

Her face was unlined, and unblemished. Her skin was pasty white, as if she had never gotten tanned in her life. He noticed that as she floated in front of him, her gills remained well under the water, and she kept dunking her mouth so they could work.

"Who are you? Where are you from?" Oslan asked, excited at the prospect of being able to actually hear what she had to say in a way that was safe for them both. She tilted her head up so her mouth could work above the water, and began to talk to him in a voice that was now less gasping and more gurgling. It made him feel almost like he had a liquid lump in his own throat as she spoke.

"My name is Placuna, and I thank you for saving me. My kingdom owes you a great debt once again. I knew that I had made the right choice in coming to you." As she spoke, she scratched absently at her arm, then realizing what she was doing, she let her hand float away from the spot. "I must get back to the ocean soon, my people are not attuned to freshwater," she explained. From the way that she looked down, Oslan would have thought that she was embarrassed, but no rosy flush came to her cheeks. When she looked up, she went on.

"Years before either of us were born, your father saved my mother's life on the Ocean of Empathy. His ship was passing a smaller fishing vessel, which had hauled my mother on board with part of their catch. You see, she had gotten caught in the fishermen's net, and never having seen a mermaid like her before, the men were preparing to bring her back to land to show anyone who would listen to them about the amazing creature they had found. But your father saw her floundering on the deck and ordered them to throw her back. When they didn't move quickly enough, he boarded their vessel and cut her from the net himself." Placuna paused in her storytelling to dunk her head under the water. Refreshed, she resurfaced to rejoin the king, still keeping her gills where she could breathe.

"I am the daughter of Destan and Mayan, the king and queen of Eathelyn. Our kingdom lies deep at the bottom of the ocean, and still today, it was known by very few men. Since the day that my mother was saved, we have followed the dealings of your kingdom by listening to travellers that pass in boats on the waves above us. Earlier this year when your ship took up port on the island off the shores of Ethik, we were there. We saw the giant dragon's shadow fly over the waves to where you were. We watched it come as each of its heads spouted flames or other things to harm you. But there was nothing we could do. Now though, I have found a way that we can repay our debt. I have news that could help, and I wanted to come to warn you."

Oslan was mesmerized by her tale. He felt a pang of sadness and pride when she talked about his father, and the noble deed he had performed.

"My father has been gone for quite some time now," he told her gently. "He had always been a hero to me." He noticed her beginning to scratch at her side, and decided to speed things up so that she could return home. "What is it that you have come to tell me?"

"Our people know of your capture of the Almatraek Dim and your search for the Almatraek Bright." She spoke cautiously, as if seeking confirmation for the facts that they had been assuming to be true.

"Yes, we have been unable to destroy the Almatraek Dim, and we are hoping that the

Almatraek Bright will be able to tell us how to do it successfully," he confided. "It was a spell from that book that killed my father, and I won't have any more of my kingdom's people suffer from the spells that lie within it. My mage and queen believes that though there may only be one dark book, it would be wise for us to make copies of the antidotes in case we should find ourselves under attack from one of its evil enchantments again. After all, the spells had to have come from somewhere. I'm sure that at least some of those mages are still out there." Relief washed over Placuna's face as he talked about copying the book.

"The Almatraek Bright is kept hidden by a brotherhood of mages who don't want to see it destroyed," she enlightened him. "For three generations, my people guarded its secrets, until my great great grandmother was spotted as a young girl playing in the waves by a boat sailing by. The next day, a Carrier of Brightness came to the palace to collect the book. They were afraid that the discovery of my kind would lead to people trying to search for the kingdom to find more of us. They decided that it was just tempting fate to continue to keep the great tome there. It was transported across the kingdom, and for more than a half a century, it has been left in the care of the dwarves of Mount Embalk. Word has already been sent that your Lazelan has been searching for it. They understand that eventually, he will go there to seek it out, so a Carrier will likely have already been dispatched to move it once again."

"But why won't they just let us have it?" Oslan brooded in frustration.

"Because of the prophecy." she answered. "They believe that only the Light Bringer will be able to avoid certain doom. The only way to destroy the

Almatraek Dim, is to cast a spell and bring the two sister books together. But in doing so, both will be wiped clean."

"That sounds straightforward enough. Aylan can copy the book and then put the books together." He decided.

"It's not that simple," she shook her head sadly. "When the books touch, it will create a wave of power that will emanate from the joining. The spell needs an immense amount of life-force to work. Everyone caught in the blast will have their energy drained to the point that they will lose all magic ability, and even their lives. The Light Bringer is said to be the only one that can join the two without being harmed. That man or woman is the only one that the Carriers of Brightness will ever relinquish the book to willingly." She looked at him expectantly, as if trying to convey more than she was actually saying out loud.

"Are you suggesting that we might have to take it by force?" Oslan asked.

"You'd never win," she rejected the idea immediately. "If the dwarves knew what you were planning, they would likely help the Carrier to stop your man. You see, only a mage would seek the book, and there would be no way for them to know if the mage in question had made copies of the Almatraek Dim, and was only seeking the hidden sister book in order to wipe *it* clean. If anyone did that, wiped out all of the antidotes and counter spells to the Almatraek Dim, it would give them an unstoppable rein of terror that could end with them ensnaring the world. The Light Bringer is the only one that they believe is pure enough to have it, and until he or she reveals themselves, anyone on the side of good will fight to protect the tome from thievery.

"Could we have Lazelan pose as this Light Bringer in order to get the book?" he suggested rapidly. His mind was on a roll now, trying to tactically come up with solutions.

"It won't work," she clarified, "The Light Bringer will only make themself known by revealing themself in the making of a miracle. He or she will gather followers. They are supposed to bring a lot of disbelievers from the darkness into a world of enlightened brightness."

"Then it is all but hopeless. How does one fake a miracle?" he probed.

"You don't have to," she replied. "The Carrier hasn't left the mountain yet. That means that the book is still hidden somewhere in one of the rooms. Your only chance is to have your man beat the Carrier to the book, and then get out without anyone noticing. You need someone who won't draw attention, a person that can be sneaky, discrete, and quiet."

(

Chapter 23
O Making An Entrance O

"Ah!" Wolfbane's ongoing tremendous scream of fear echoed off the mountains as they plummeted toward the rock and snow. The sphinxes' wings were plastered back against their furry sides to reduce drag as they dove downward to a place where they could safely land. Lazelan feared that Wolfbane was going to soil himself, although with how much stock the two giant flying cats put in this Jarusiyat business, he was pretty sure that they wouldn't blame him even if he did. Lazelan had to admit that their speed was intense. It almost seemed like the mountain was rushing up to meet them instead of them flying to it. He gritted his teeth and bore down on his gut to try to keep his stomach from leaping up into his throat. The speed of their fall was so awesome that in the last few seconds, he had to turn his face sideways into the thick sand-coloured fur of the giant cat. For good measure, he also screwed his eyes shut just so he didn't reflexively cast a spell to halt their decent.

Seconds before impact, the sphinx's wings unfurled, catching the air in them like two great sails on a ship. The upper half of the cat Lazelan was riding seemed to stop dead in the air, while his back half swung down gracefully, hind toes and claws splayed in order to touch down and find purchase. To Lazelan, who was sitting up by the sphinxes neck and shoulders, it had felt like being slammed into a furry brick wall by a rather large troll. He groaned and raised a hand to his head where the impact had produced a headache. He was pretty sure that one of the sphinxes was chuckling under its breath.

Lazelan and Wolfbane slid off of the backs of the great beasts that had flown them so far.

"We must return to the pyramid. There is no telling what kind of riffraff might have tried to enter the pyramid in our absence. Besides, we sphinxes are acclimated to the Embralic Desert, and this snow is too much." As if to accentuate her point, she flicked a paw and the glob of snow that came free would have hit Lazelan smartly upside the head had he not been quick enough to cast a small shield. One thing was for sure, these cats had certainly kept him on his toes.

"We are sorry that we can serve you no longer," the male added, "But the cold makes it difficult for us to use our wings." He flapped them stiffly once, and a giant feather came loose and see-sawed lazily to the snow.

"Yes, this is the way of it," the female smiled sadly. "May brightness be behind you on your quest."

"And be with you on yours," Lazelan responded automatically. He bowed deeply at the waist out of respect for the half-felines. He didn't know how he and the gnome would have gotten here without them.

Wolfbane nodded to both cats in thanks. "I guess you'd better fly before you *Cat*ch cold."

"That would be a *cat*astrophe," the male sphinx grinned.

"Yes," the female agreed, "when he gets sick, he lays around in a positively *cat*atonic state. Can't do a thing with him."

Wolfbane hugged her giant paw fondly and stepped back to allow them to go. They flapped their massive wings, turning up swirls of snow around the gnome and mage, and took off into the cold blue sky.

Once the sphinxes had become specks in the distance, Lazelan and Wolfbane turned to the entranceway to the mountain. The wood of the crimson double doors rose to form a peak where they joined together. Wolfbane stared up at them, slack-jawed.

"All of the dwarves that I've ever met were only slightly taller than me," he stated in wonder. "Are mountain dwarves any bigger than normal?"

"Not that I have heard," Lazelan answered warily. He had noticed the two gargoyles crouching in the alcoves near the doors. They appeared to be statues. They were ugly, but that wasn't what was preoccupying his mind. It was the upper two alcoves that were empty that had stolen his attention. They looked as though they should have held statues as well.

Wolfbane was still going on about the doors that towered over them. The doors hadn't worried Lazelan at all until his gnomish friend got to the point.

"Assuming that mountain dwarves are the same as any other that we've met, then why are the doors big enough to admit something the size of a troll?"

Lazelan's stomach sank. Trolls were supposed to be unruly creatures with a constantly sour disposition. Lazelan was tall for a man, but if the books he had studied were correct, then his nest of fiery red curls would only sit at mid-thigh on a troll. They had better find a peaceful way to gain admittance into the mountain. It would zap most of Lazelan's energy to fight something the size of a troll, no matter what it was, and he didn't see anything around that he could draw more energy from aside from Wolfbane. Lazelan felt bile rise in his throat as he got the feeling that things were about to go very wrong. He dipped into his energy pool, at the ready.

"I feel like we're being watched, but there's no-one he-" Wolfbane's words were cut off by the sound of a couple of quick leathery flaps behind and above them.

"Krakuai kaeja nula taek!" *Powerful gust of air!* Lazelan shouted as he whirled and sent forth a concentrated blast of wind fit to knock down a troll-sized being.

Time seemed to slow the way it sometimes did in the middle of a horrific accident or an intense battle. Lazelan got a glimpse of the the gnarled stony beast being propelled toward him on bat-like wings. Its fingertips were carved into rocky points like claws that reached out in his direction either to tear at or to capture the mage. For a moment, Lazelan watched its evil-looking face grinning intently at him, then as the blast hit it, the expression was wiped clean and replaced with surprise and panic.

Lazelan's gust hit the gargoyle's widespread wings. They instantly caught the air, making them inadvertently billow out like shirts on a clothesline before the force thrust the thing back. It spun head over heels through the air, and it let out a rather human sounding cry as it went. It landed some distance away, disappearing into the deep snow.

Lazelan turned immediately to the other two gargoyles that remained by the sides of the doors. They were as still as statues no longer, but they made no move to leave their alcoves. In fact one was chuckling in a low gravelly voice as he peered after his fallen comrade, and the other of the pair was giving the mage an appreciative slow applause. Apparently, they were smart enough not to want to fight a mage without having been provoked first. Lazelan thought that would end though when he tried to open one of the doors.

Now the other airborne gargoyle came swooping down over the ledge of a higher cliff, and headed straight for the gnome. Wolfbane straightened and went for his fiery scimitar.

"Don't worry, Lazelan, I've got this one." He pulled out his sword, the curved blade blazing to life as it left the sheath. Wolfbane held it up impressively to show the attacking gargoyle. His stance was not of one ready for fighting, he was merely waiting for the creature to stop dead in its tracks as the sphinxes had.

The gargoyle pulled up short as it got close and noticed the inferno apparently burning from the blade itself. Wolfbane relaxed, and his stance became cocky.

"Behold," he told the gargoyle as he began to wave the sword majestically from side to side. "I am the chos-"

The gargoyle showed no sign of recognition or humility. Instead, it simply slapped the menacing sword out of Wolfbane's hand, and lunged at the disarmed gnome.

The scimitar hit the snow six feet away with a hiss as the blade instantly turned the snow that was touching it to steam. Wolfbane yelped and he dove for it, landing on his belly and narrowly missing being caught in the gargoyle's clutches as the stony arms passed through the space he had just occupied. The heat from the blade was melting the snow at a frightening rate, and Wolfbane began digging in the snow frantically as the sword got away from him, passing deeper and deeper through the layers of frigid white.

The stony beast went for the gnome again and seized his boot at the very instant that Wolfbane got one hand around the hilt. The thing cried out in victory as he lifted the small man up off the snow by the ankle. As it did, the sword came up with the gnome, but it no longer burned.

"You extinguished my sword!" the upside down gnome lamented. "You better not have broken it, I loved that thing! Luckily, it still looks sharp." With that, he began to try to slash at the gargoyle that was holding him.

Lazelan watched the exchange in frustration. He couldn't get a clear shot at the gargoyle with Wolfbane there, so he held onto the coil of energy, waiting for his window of opportunity. *Brains are always better than brawn*, one of his professors at the university had always said. *For almost any situation that demands a fight, you could think your way out of instead*, he had always professed. It was a wholly understandable stance coming from the man who was a bookish tiny fellow with a timid mouse-like demeanor. He had always worn a big round pair of glasses that had made the man reminiscent of an owl. Even so, the man had not been wrong.

Lazelan was sure that there had been a dwarf from these parts that had attended the university too. His professor had even mentioned him in some of their classes together. He had been a mage that had done some amazing things with his magic in relation to gemstones. Now if Lazelan could only call up the name.

Wolfbane still hung in the grasp of the large stone gargoyle, seemingly at an impasse. He kept trying to plunge the sword into its body, but the gargoyle's arm was long enough that it held Wolfbane at a safe distance away from itself. That having been said, it couldn't do anything with the gnome except hold it, for if the thing were to bring Wolfbane close enough to slash at him with his free claws, the gnome might get a lucky shot in.

"A little help here?" Wolfbane called to the mage.

"I'm working on it, I assure you." Lazelan told him. "Do you know anything about dwarves and gemstones?"

"Other than the fact that dwarves mine them? No." the dangling gnome answered in between swipes at the beast holding him.

Drat, Lazelan cursed to himself. He hadn't really expected his friend to know, but it had been worth a shot. He ran through the prof's lesson in his mind. The dwarven mage had somehow harnessed the power of a spell in a gemstone, so that it could be triggered under certain conditions. It was similar to the way that the fire in Wolfbane's sword worked. The dwarf's name was right on the tip of his tongue. *Boldrash? No. Balderdash? Not quite. Bolderrig? That wasn't it, but it was similar.*

"Boudlerdig!" he exclaimed triumphantly. He spoke to the two lounging gargoyles. "We are here to see Demar Boulderdig, if he's still alive."

"Well, why didn't you say so?" the one holding Wolfbane asked as he unceremoniously dropped him on his head into the snow.

The two in the alcoves perked up, and one used the side of a stony fist to pound a secret rhythm on one of the giant doors.

Almost instantly, as if someone had been waiting on the other side, there came the sound of a bolt sliding out of a great lock.

Lazelan looked up, power still held at the ready, unsure of whether he was going to face a giant mountain dwarf, or a hungry hulking troll that waited behind the now opening doors.

Chapter 24
O Midriff Mischief O

For the first time in weeks, a span that had really felt like months, Sasha was able to slip into a trance with no trouble at all. There was no sign of the eclipsing darkness that had been plaguing her ability to see, and the relief she felt was almost tangible. As her dreams and visions solidified, swirled, and then came together to show her something new, she realized that she felt free.

However, the visions that she was having made worry crease her brow as she saw one attack after another. She caught a snippet of a great dark blur racing toward Lazelan's back. Right before it got to him, the mage turned with his hands outstretched, and whatever the thing was suddenly flew backwards away from him.

Next, she saw the king with a beautiful girl. She had her arms wrapped around him in a way that was decidedly not proper, but something was wrong with the scene. Gravity seemed to have gone, as their hair hair and clothes floated around them, weightless. That is when she saw the bubble escape from Oslan's lips to float upward, making Sasha realized that they must be under water. The king was trying to swim to the surface, but the girl was holding him under.

The vision died and was replaced by Wolfbane, dashing in his green breastplate, but being held upside down by a stony creature a head and a half taller than an average man. Wolfbane was struggling and slashing out with his weapon, but his sword couldn't seem to land a hit.

Then her dreams brought her back to the palace. Aylan sat on her throne, perhaps seeing petitioners, and everything seemed to be going normally. That is until a boy approached the dais. Sasha recognized him immediately. She had often seen him out in the garden speaking with Sabyn. She couldn't recall his name though. She would have to remember to ask her handmaid what it was when she woke. In her vision, he held a woven wicker basket in his hands. A sprig of some kind of flower or twig was poking out of it. The queen rose from the throne and came to meet him. He handed her the basket and she fell toward the ground. Oslan caught her, and she saw a knight begin to clear the room.

The scene tilted, came apart, and changed into something new. Everything was black. There was an unnatural and complete absence of light. At first Sasha was startled, thinking that the eclipse had come upon her again, and was total this time. She felt a pang of anguish, thinking that her ability might have left her completely. With her wits on edge, there was the faintest wisp of a whisper. Then a searing bright light pierced the darkness of her vision. It started as a sliver and grew into a brilliant fire that revealed two faces. One was Wolfbane's, and the other was that of a bald stranger. Other terrified faces surrounded them as the two visages seemed to size each other up.

Sasha's vision was violently ripped apart as an unknown person attempted to shake the seer awake. Someone was calling her name, but she couldn't find her way back to full consciousness. Having visions wasn't the same as dreaming; she was down deeper in her subconscious, using parts of her brain that perhaps others were not able to access. When down so deep, it wasn't a matter of waking up, one had to come out of a trance gradually, rising through the almost viscous levels of unconsciousness and coming to the surface of where conscious thought could occur. Being forcibly woken while having a vision, was like having a heart attack while trying to swim through molasses. The thick substance was so dark that you wouldn't really know which way was up.

Her name came to her ears through the depths again. Whoever was calling her sounded frantic. Sasha felt disoriented and lost. She began to count in her head, willing her conscious mind to rise through up and out of the darkness. With each number, came clarity and more awareness of her surroundings.

"Sasha, by all that is bright, wake up!" She could hear it clearly now. It was Millie's despairing voice. But why wasn't she with the queen?

As Sasha finally reached the last number in her counting, it was like a diver finally bringing their head above water. She opened her light brown eyes. She was shaking. Such a traumatic awakening could put a person into shock, and Sasha was attempting to fight it while listening to the gush of words that began spilling out of the queen's lady-in-waiting the second that Sasha opened her eyes.

"I'm sorry for disturbing you, but Aylan has put us all in danger, and I needed to bring someone that would understand."

This was alarming news indeed. She looked over to Sabyn's sleeping palate, but the girl was missing. "Please pour me a drink of water," she instructed the other girl as she sat up, "Then tell me exactly what has happened."

"Now's no time for drinks, Milady, you should come right away."

"Millie, you have woken me from a trance. Doing this is very dangerous for a seer." She held her hand up parallel to the floor. The hand was visibly aquiver. I need to steady myself before I can go anywhere, and the mundane task of drinking a cup of water will help a lot."

The other girl clasped her hands in front of her, blushed, and looked down contritely.

"I'm sorry, Sasha, I didn't know. Please forgive me." It was quite the change from when Aylan had first been given the girl as a handmaid, and had found the girl snooping through her things. After years of service, Millie had mellowed into a very respectful servant. The girl went to the outer room, and Sasha heard water being poured.

Millie returned and handed the cup to Sasha. Then she stood nearby, anxiously shifting her weight from one foot to the other as the seer drank. It was obvious that she was trying to give Sasha the time she needed to come completely to her senses, but the feeling of urgency hadn't left the girl.

"Why don't you tell me what happened?" Sasha offered.

At first Millie seemed reluctant to say anything. Instead, she looked anxiously toward the door, licked her lips, and looked back to Sasha. *The poor girl must be spooked, she looks as if she's going to bolt at any second*, Sasha realized.

"Go on," she coaxed, "What did the queen do that was so dangerous?" the seer asked. She was pretty sure that whatever it was, the girl was likely just over reacting.

Millie licked her lips out of nervousness again. Then reluctantly she said, "It wasn't so much Aylan as the baby."

"The baby?" Sasha asked, now worried. "What happened to the baby?"

"Nothing happened to it, it's what the infant did." the girl explained gingerly while glancing at the door again.

Sasha remembered seeing Wolfbane hovering above the stool as the child's hijacked spell had kept him there. *The unborn child is beginning to be like a wild card in a game of Kingdom; it could change everything, and we have no warning as to when its effects will pop up.* Sasha thought, irritated.

"The baby sort of set fire to the castle!" Millie blurted out.

"What?" Sasha exclaimed in alarm.

"I guess the baby woke before Aylan did," she started, "It must have kicked her while the queen slept, because she sort of groaned in her sleep. She rolled over and would have fallen right off the bed, but she just hung there beside the bed, two feet off the ground."

"The baby saved Aylan from falling?" Sasha asked incredulously.

"Or it saved itself," Millie confirmed. "Although, I suppose it just has an affinity for her levitation spell. Perhaps it's the only one it knows how to use."

"We might be lucky there," Sasha said grimly. "But where does the fire come in?"

"When Aylan was hovering there, I couldn't believe my eyes. I thought that mayhap I had nodded off while sitting by the bed. So I lit another candle to make sure that I was actually seeing what I thought I had seen. It floated up off the table, and across the room, and all the while the flame flickered as it went. It didn't seem to be going anywhere in particular; it just sort of floated around. I tried to grab hold of it and pull it out of the air, but the spell was so strong that when I held on, it began to drag me along with it. I let go and it kind of sprung forward into the curtain beside the window." Millie had leaned forward toward Sasha as her voice dropped with each word until at the end it came out in only a whisper. Sasha's arms had broken out in gooseflesh, and she tried to ignore the icy fingers of fear that were drawing trails up her spine.

"How were you able to get the blaze out?" Sasha demanded. She knew that the other girl wouldn't be here if the fire had gotten out of hand.

"I ran to Aylan to try to get her to wake up. I managed to push her all the way back onto the bed, but she slumbered on." the lady-in-waiting told her. "So I called for the guard at his post outside in the corridor, and he came in, yanked the curtain off the wall and used part of it to smother the flames."

"This is getting worse and worse." Sasha lamented. "The baby has actually used a spell on the queen herself? She is lucky that it was only a levitate spell. We have to do something to convince her not to use her magic to give it more abilities."

"I know that Lazelan said that she should try not to cast, but she's getting ready to do so right now," Millie informed her. "Oslan has returned. He swept into the room while the curtain was still smoking in the guard's hands. He sat the queen up and dabbed at her face with a wet cloth to wake her. When she came to, he let her know that he brought urgent news with him. He asked her to try to scry Lazelan with a warning."

"We can't let her!" Sasha warned, "Lazelan is surely at Mount Embalk by now. That is as far to the northwest as our kingdom goes! If the baby attempts to keep her spell going, it could kill her!"

"I know, I came to fetch you the moment that she began waddling her way to her laboratory." Millie told her. Sasha stood and rushed to the door.

"Then we must run."

☾

Chapter 25
O Not Very Bright O

After being checked over and having been deemed to have recovered, Odal was allowed to go. Nalvo left him to change, and promised that he would be waiting for him when he was ready. Odal felt a pang of regret at having to doff the comfortable pajamas he had awoken in. Although he wasn't one to throw money around, he found himself wanting to splurge a little in order to get an equally luxurious outfit for himself.

He undid the few buttons at the neck of his night shirt, and lifted it over his head. The mountain's chilly air licked at his body, making him move a little faster to get his own clothes back on. He found everything from his knitted woolen stockings to his coat folded on the desk. All had been dried, presumably by magic.

His layers of warm woolly wear went on, shutting out the room's cold piece by piece. He was just tying his brown, gold, and black sash around his waist when Nalvo blew into the room without the courtesy of a single knock.

"Do you mind? I was just getting dressed! What if I had been naked?" Odal shrieked like a scandalized maid.

"Oh, Odal, if I had walked in on you unclad to the hide, then I suppose I would have learned my lesson. As it is, I've never been one to knock on my own doors, and quite honestly, I probably won't start now. The only thing wrong with your attire is that you've got your beard stuck in your sash." He answered candidly.

Odal looked down and saw the tips of his thick brownish-red beard sticking straight out from under his sash like the tongue of a brazen young lad. He grabbed his beard above the sash in a meaty fist and yanked it out with one hasty pull.

Nalvo grabbed him by the arm and started to usher him hurriedly toward the door. "We must make haste, Odal, there was a commotion at the door and whoever it was has been let in."

"But surely, the guards will have dealt with any problems," Odal reasoned.

"Yes, yes, of course." the other dwarf agreed, "But we're on the welcoming committee."

"When did this happen? I've never heard of such a thing." Odal protested as he was dragged into the hallway and propelled down the corridor by Nalvo's continual pulling.

"I just made one up," Nalvo informed him, "and for us to have an official committee there has to be at least two of us. The guards reported the use of magic out there. Maybe it's another Carrier of Brightness! This could be two in one day, what are the chances of that? We're going to get to meet them both!"

Odal tried to stop short, but it was no use. It was usually hard for an opponent to move a dwarf once they planted themselves firmly to the ground, however, Nalvo's constant movement wasn't giving Odal a chance to find his stance. He stumbled instead.

"Oh, do try to keep up!" Nalvo chided heavily. "I wonder why they'd send two. Well, really, I wonder why Maewyn came at all. Sending two seems kind of excessive. Not that I'm complaining, you understand."

"Who's Maewyn?" Odal interrupted. Nalvo sighed impatiently.

"Maewyn Azemar is only the Carrier of Brightness that Dain is probably boring to death at this very minute. We're on a first name basis,

Maewyn and I." Nalvo reported proudly. "Anyway, the moment I introduced Dain to Maewyn, the two of them went off to speak with each other, and undoubtedly Dain has already taken the opportunity to give the Carrier the invitation of the emerald hall."

"So this time you're going to make sure to offer the lodgings of the sapphire hall to this newcomer to ensure that a Carrier will be staying with you, too." Odal guessed.

"Precisely," Nalvo confirmed as they left the tunnels of the sapphire veins and entered the precious gathering of colours of the grand hall.

Today it stood with all seats empty, although there was no lack of people in the cavern as an impressive conglomeration of dwarves bustled here and there with armloads of decorations. Teams of dwarves worked together with pulleys and swings set around the walls. One dwarf would take up an ornament and sit on the swing, and the rest would pull the other end of the rope to hoist the swing into the air. There were hooks on the walls to allow for hanging, and once at it, the process never took very long. Green adornments were going up everywhere. Apparently the emerald clan was preparing the hall for a feast of some sort, and Odal had a good idea of who it was in honor of. He began to fall behind, and realized that Nalvo had picked up his pace as soon as they had entered the hallway on the other side.

They followed the veinless tunnel that lead to the doorway, paying attention to the chiseled dwarven runes that marked each offshoot and shaft so they didn't get lost in the maze of halls on the way. Three cities lay within this mountain, and all were ancient and connected by several layers of catacombs and passageways that numbered in the hundreds. Only a handful were relatively new within the last ten generations, and many existed that had been long forgotten. If not for the runes that marked where each ended or intersected, a dwarf could get lost in the mines forever. Some that had been illiterate actually had.

At last, the echoes of conversing voices came to meet their ears as they hurried along. The light around the next bend became brighter as they entered the cavern where the giant red doors lay opened, letting in the sun light.

Odal threw up his arm to shield his eyes from the stinging assault, as Nalvo shouted "Shut the doors!"

Odal could make out the silhouettes of a small group of people that stood there, talking. Two of the members jumped at the sound of Nalvo's command, and ran to begin closing the doors.

"Nalvo, Odal!" one guard acknowledged them, "We were giving their eyes time to adjust."

Odal thought that Nalvo looked slightly abashed at not having thought about the procedure they had in place out of courtesy for their very infrequent visitors. Normally when a sun soaker entered, the doors would be closed by degrees over a number of minutes so as not to blind the newcomer completely. It was a gentler sort of welcome.

"Of course, of course," the half-blind Nalvo acquiesced, as he willed his eyes to function properly in the brilliant rays that split the comfortable darkness.

Odal went to their hooks and grabbed the pair of goggles he had worn outside to save his own eyes. They seemed to relax at once in relief as he slipped the tinted gems on.

"They are here to see Demar," the guard informed the clan chiefs.

Nalvo was half way to the rack to get his own goggles when the guard spoke, and now he turned abruptly at the mention of Demar's name. Not only was he one of the few mages within the halls of the mountain dwarves, but he was also Dain's brother. Nalvo rushed over to the newcomers and shook their hands, introducing himself and not letting them get a word in edgewise.

"My name is Nalvo Foespear, and I want to take this opportunity to welcome you to Mount Embalk. One of your brothers is already here and has agreed to stay with the emerald clan, but I would like to extend an even warmer invitation for you two esteemed Carriers to stay with me within the walls of the sapphire clan." Without letting them answer, he said, "Good, now that that is settled, we can go find Demar."

Odal tried to suppress a chuckle as he watched the surprised and almost horrified looks on the faces of the two sun soakers that stood before them as their hands were pumped and arrangements were made on their behalf. Now, Nalvo finally got his goggles, and putting them on, saw what the pair actually looked like.

These two were not dressed at all like the other Carrier of Brightness. For one, neither had the shaved head of a male Carrier; the tall gangly one had red curly hair that looked windblown to the extreme. The short one, obviously a gnome, was clearly not even a mage, with his breastplate of green armour and multiple swords at his side. Both looked dishevelled and battle-worn. Likely, one was a grunt sent to protect the other, who was likely a simple messenger. As if to prove the point, neither wore the Carriers of Brightness' required gold chain or holy symbol of a bright burning torch.

Nalvo's jaw dropped open at the sight of them. To Odal, the devastated expression on the other dwarf's face was almost worth being left in the snow earlier.

(

Chapter 26
○ The Way of a Wench ○

Sasha outpaced Millie only slightly as they rounded the corner to the hall where the armoury lay. Their movements attracted the eye of the guards that stood sentinel outside the solid double doors. They immediately stood up a little straighter, and puffed out their chests to seem larger. Their polished suits of armour glinted and shone impressively in the torch light from the walls.

Sasha was used to this type of behaviour, at least from men, anyway. She was widely considered to be one of the most beautiful ladies in Endalwynndale, the news of which had spread mainly because of her unusual height. Minstrels that had come to the castle had left writing songs about the beauteous lady with golden hair like the sun, perfect creamy complexion, and the lofty height of a a tree. Obviously, the last had been grossly exaggerated, but at least they weren't comparing her to a man, which was closer to the truth.

These songs had brought with them a long line of suitors that had all been rejected. That meant that she was still single, and all of the eligible men knew it. The up side of this for Sasha was that it meant that she usually always got her way with the male nobles and knights alike. For some reason, however, these two were still barring her way into the armoury. Drawing closer, she realized that she didn't recognize them, and they in turn, wouldn't know who she was. This could mean trouble.

Both were older than the normal palace guards. The one on the left had short fluffy white hair, laugh lines, and alert green eyes. The other to the right appeared to be slightly younger, with his collar-length hair still mostly black and hard eyes the colour of mud.

The urgency of the need to get through the door they were blocking chaffed at Sasha. *I can't take this right now!* her mind wailed. *We have to get through!* But with an effort, she kept her face friendly, and her voice calm. If they heard any alarm in it, it might alert them that something was up. Then even if they managed to get in, she didn't want them poking their heads in on her and Millie once they were inside.

"Do excuse us, gentlemen, but we really must enter." she announced, indicating the door they were standing in front of.

"I'm sorry, Milady, but only knights or those accompanied by the king or queen may pass," he informed her. "Ever since that herbologist hypnotized that poor lad in order to rob the nobles, security in the castle has been doubled. The only way we could let you through without King Oslan or Queen Aylan would be if you were here on royal business." Each guard held a long spear in the hand that rested between them. As if on cue, and to reinforce what the guard was saying, both extended their arms toward one another so that the spears crossed right where the double doors met.

They really aren't going to let us in! she lamented. She was caught off-guard. She really had never encountered a situation like this before and didn't know how to handle it. *Perhaps I can flirt my way in. I've seen women at the tavern flirt before. Surely, it can't be that hard.*

She tried to be graceful. The way she normally moved was elegant and fluid, everything a lady should be, but then she wasn't thinking about it. What happened now as she attempted to approach the guard on the right, was just awkward.

Rising up on her toes to walk daintily, her ankle rolled and she stumbled right into him. His free arm came up around her waist to steady her, and she decided to use that to her advantage.

"Oh, thank you, and please, my name is Sasha." she cooed in what she considered to be a rather annoying higher register that one reserved for talking to babies and froofy dogs. The sound was grating to her own ears, but it seemed to work for the wenches in the pub.

She placed a light hand on the guard's shoulder as she came down off her toes. It was not appropriate for a lady to be so familiar with a gentleman that she was not betrothed to, and out of respect, the knight immediately removed his hand from around her waist, returning to his normal stance. He cleared his throat.

"I am Sir Reginald," he stated cordially. "Excuse me for saying so, Lady Sasha, but perhaps you have enjoyed just a bit too much spiced wine?" He seemed to be actively trying to ignore the warm body leaning into his armour.

Darn, this isn't working! she realized in frustration. She really didn't know what she was doing, but in for a copper, in for a purse. *I'll have to lay it on thicker,* she decided. She began to curl a strand of her waist-long golden tresses around her finger in a coquettish way.

"I think I may have, *Sir* Reginald. I suddenly seem to be rather unsteady on my feet." this last sentence came out sounding just a tad sarcastically. She hoped that he hadn't noticed. She covered it up with a simpering giggle. She tried very hard to coo once again. "Perhaps a strong man such as yourself could help me to a chair. There happen to be several in the war room." She finished by looking deeply into his eyes while trying to flutter her lashes.

He seemed slightly alarmed. "I do apologize, but there is simply no way that I allow you in there."

She saw him finally notice her eyelashes fluttering as she continued to blink rapidly at him. He looked deeply into her eyes, his gaze switching back and forth from one of her light brown irises to the other. She watched as his mud-brown eyes glanced down at her puckering lips. That's when she realized that her breathing had seemed to have sped up. His eyes softened and she saw recognition don on him like a lever being thrown. His gauntlet-clad hand came up to the spot on her waist where he had steadied her before. She could feel the heat from his palm through her gown. He bent his face closer to her to speak softly so the others would not hear.

"Lady Sasha," he breathed her name in a low husky whisper. "Are you having a fit?"

Sasha gave up. She blew out her bangs and straightened up, stepping away from the knight quite steadily.

"Please ignore that, Sir Reginald, I can assure you that I am of sound body and mind." she declared in her normal musical tones, if a little crisply.

That is when Millie saved the day. "I am Queen Aylan's lady-in-waiting, Millie. She has gone into the war room, and has asked me to follow with a cool cloth to sooth her head." She presented a piece of material all wrapped up like a compress.

"Oh, of course, Millie, go right in." As he spoke, both men pulled their spears away from the centre of the door and stepped away from each other to admit the women. "Queen Aylan entered earlier with the king. I would suggest knocking once you get to the war room door, in case they are discussing plans of a sensitive nature."

He actually tipped the lady-in-waiting a wink as the women passed by. Once they were inside, Sasha asked the maid, "Where did you get that? Do you always walk around carrying a wet cloth?"

Millie laughed and unfurled the material to reveal that it was rectangular and had some ties. "It's dry. In fact, it's nothing more than my apron."

Sasha had to smile at the maid's ingenuity. They hurried into the war room, and went in behind the tapestry that led the way to Aylan's secret work room. Now that they were out of the sight of potentially prying eyes, they hiked up their skirts and ran as fast as they could so they could warn Aylan of what might happen if she cast a new spell that could potentially cover a long distance.

A painful stitch began to sear in Sasha's side as she ran, and she found herself gulping for air. Millie threw her a concerned look, but Sasha shook her head and kept on going, refusing to slow. She would have time to stop in a few moments once they got there. This was way too important. She doubted that she would have halted even if the castle walls had started to come down around them. Aylan was her very best friend, and she wasn't about to lose her.

The door was in sight now. The heels of the women's slippers echoed off the stone walls as they hustled up the hall to the stairs. They were up them in a flash, and Sasha called ahead just before they burst into the laboratory without stopping to knock.

"Aylan, whatever you do, you mustn't scry!"

They rushed in to find Oslan staring quizzically in their direction and Aylan still facing the gigantic gilt-edged mirror that the queen favoured for scrying. Sasha's heart had been pounding in her chest like the hooves of a galloping stallion, but now it seemed to stop for a moment. If she had seen the royal couple's reflection on the mirror's surface, it might not have been too late. But as it was, there was no likeness of them at all, only the image of Lazelan standing in a brightly lit rocky room leagues away on the other side of the kingdom.

Chapter 27
O Hide and Seek O

Lazelan and Wolfbane had been escorted by the two Dwarves through tunnels that had been expertly hewn to form smooth corridors. At first, the wide walls and high curving ceiling had just been the expected dull grey stone. The mountain was cold, and neither Lazelan nor Wolfbane were dressed for it. Goosebumps stood out on the mage's whole body now, and he kept walking quickly to try to warm himself up. Mercifully though, the tunnels were dry, and not dank in the least.

They passed into an intersection of shafts that was as large as a small inn's common room. It was almost as if the rock had been cut away in a half-bubble. Lazelan reached up to feel the cool surface of the rock, so smooth that it felt like glass under his fingertips. Magic left no residual sign that it had ever been there. Perhaps how they had done it would be a mystery forever.

"The tunnels that ended up being incorporated into our living space was smoothed out by expert stoneworkers. There are places that were polished for months to get it relatively close to what could be done in an instant with a spell. Dain and Demar did a fair bit of magic when these tunnels were being made." Odal informed them. "Only where they came together, you understand. To use magic to cut new mineshafts would be foolhardy, you see. Removing a large chunk of the mountain all at once could make us miss where the gemstone runs. Then we would run the risk of tunneling in the wrong direction." His voice was beginning to take on the instructional voice of one who had given the same lecture a number of times. "But they were able to follow the ways of our ancestors to widen areas like these so that foot traffic didn't get congested while we worked in the mines."

Branching off from this space were five corridors. One was still incredibly large, with a ceiling as big as the gigantic doors that had first admitted them. The rest however, were much smaller and narrower, only wide enough to admit three dwarves abreast. Nalvo cleared his throat impatiently. Lazelan was pretty sure that Odal rolled his eyes, but it was hard to tell for sure in the dim light. Odal consulted a set of runes chiseled into the wall beside the openings, and indicated the third short tunnel with a sweep of his arm, and they continued on their way. Lazelan was fairly tall for a man, standing just over six feet. The ceiling here only gave his head a two inch clearance. It gave him a weird sensation of the mountain pressing down on his spine, which made him feel a flinching need to duck. He supposed that for the two dwarves, who stood only a head taller than Wolfbane, the ceilings would seem comfortable. After turning down several hallways, Lazelan began to see shimmering lines of colour running through the rock. Some stopped abruptly, and others ran the length of each corridor, branching off into yet more veins that sparkled and shone.

Lines of red rubies of a shade as dark as blood followed their progress. Thanks to the torches that lit their way, and the highly glossy polish of the rock, the gemstone even looked wet. Lazelan's sense of scholarly curiosity made him itch to reach up and touch it, but he refrained. Wolfbane seemed unaffected by the sheer wealth around them, which surprised the mage. The gnome was strangely quiet too.

After switching to the seventh or eighth tunnel, Lazelan noticed a vein of blue as dark as the

Ocean of Empathy, racing along beside the red one. As they continued to move, Amethysts joined the river of shimmering shades, followed by diamonds, Tigers-eye, and emerald as green as the farmlands back home in Ethik, where Lazelan's young wife, Magdolyn, waited for him.

He let his mind wander; thinking of her long hair as red as his own, her gorgeous green eyes, and her beautiful smile that could stop a man in his tracks. Maybe he could buy one of the dwarves' world-famous gemstones for her. That might lessen the sting of him being away for so long.

Paying attention to where they were going was fruitless. He had lost count of which way to turn down the twisting tunnels after the fourth intersection. He was going to have to scry with Aylan and Oslan to try to formulate a plan for how he and Wolfbane were to get back out. Perhaps the king had a map in the war room that could help them plot a course.

Murmurs of distant voices started to reach them as the sounds echoed off of the walls. As they rounded the last bend in the corridor, the cadences of conversations became sharper. Up ahead, a shaft of illumination spilled into the tunnel which began to make the light quality a bit better.

They came out into what could only be described as a ball room. Tables circled one half of the giant sparkling cavern, and a wide open space, presumably for dancing, took up the other. Lazelan was aware that Wolfbane had stopped short, and stood agape in awe. He was looking up with a twinkle in his eye, and a dreamy smile widening across his face. Lazelan realized that the massive space with jeweled walls had stunned him the same way, and he closed his own slack jawed mouth. There was more wealth in this one room than in all of the lord's treasuries in entire rest of the kingdom combined. It was like standing in the middle of a humongous polished multi-faceted geode. This space had the same rounded look as the intersections they had passed through before, and scanning the walls, Lazelan found seven passageways leading away into the mountain. Around each one, a different colour of gem seemed to leave the rest and converge around the tunnel in an arc. One was the purple of amethyst, another ruby red, white diamond, the streaking black and golds of tigers-eye, emerald green, and the last, the one that the two dwarves had continued toward, was the oceanic blue sapphire.

The mage heard the impatient clearing of the blond dwarf's throat again, and realized that he and Wolfbane had fallen behind. Lazelan clapped Wolfbane on the back to get him moving. They crossed the ballroom, and Lazelan was unable to ignore the outright stares from decorators that were hustling and bustling around the room. He imagined that they didn't get visitors all that often.

Nalvo took the lead as the two dwarves let them under the blue archway that matched the trim on the blond dwarf's heavy white coat. Lazelan made the connection, and it was like something clicked into place in the back of his mind.

They were led to a room, and although Odal stayed with them, they were left to their own devices. Nalvo excused himself, saying that he had other things to tend to. Lazelan wasted no time unshouldering his satchel and unlatched it to pull out his cloak. But as he noticed his friend's actions, he thought better of himself and dropped it on the bed. Wolfbane had begun stepping from foot to foot while he rubbed his hands up and down his arms to try to stay warm. Out of habit, Lazelan immediately looked for a fireplace to light, but of course, there were none. There would be no chimneys in a mountain to let the smoke out. They needed a heat source that required no fuel for burning, and would therefore make no smoke with which to choke them.

He brought his hands together as if holding an imaginary ball about a foot across. He pulled a small amount of energy from his core and intoned, "Wahss, fuexi, est taek, katut tari laek nula fuer." *Heat, light and air, make a sphere of fire.*

Odal cried out and turned away from the light of the fireball that instantly bloomed between Lazelan's hands. Even for Lazelan, the sudden brightness seemed to stab at his eyes, and it was almost enough for him to drop the spell. But he stood fast and kept pouring his energy into it. As the flames burned hot between his hands, the temperature in the room rose significantly and swiftly. With another quick spell, "Fli", *levitate,* and a small push from an additional trickle of power, Lazelan sent the blaze into the air to hang there further away from their eyes. He pulled back some of the energy that he was expending to keep the ball going, and it quickly dimmed as it hung in the air near the ceiling.

Lazelan's eyes almost teared up with relief, and it was now warm enough in the room for his cloak to remain forgotten for the moment on the bed. The dwarf seemed to be the uncomfortable one now, eyeing the ball of fire mistrustfully, and loosening his heavy coat where it overlapped at the front. Beads of sweat had broken out across his brow, and he had begun stroking his reddish-brown beard rhythmically as if something was bothering him.

"Are you not used to seeing magic being used?" Lazelan asked kindly. He knew that most people didn't even believe that powers beyond herbs and sleight-of-hand tricks, what mages called magic of the mind, even existed. The dwarf seemed to be sizing him up.

"Are you sure that you're not a Carrier of Brightness?" he asked in response.

Wolfbane broke out in a hearty belly laugh that went on for some time, and by the end of it, he was doubled over in two, clutching his belly with one hand and bracing himself with the other on his knee.

"I was only asking," the dwarf grumbled. Then to Lazelan, he explained, "I've only seen the Boulderdig twins use spells to make a bubble that cut away rock, and earlier today a Carrier arrived and used something similar to hold back an avalanche. I've never seen magic used many other ways. Since both Dain and Demar only seem to know the one spell, I figured that you must be far more powerful, and someone sent to keep tabs on the other Carrier, perhaps."

Lazelan was flabbergasted. This dwarf had only seen Demar use one spell? There had been a whole chapter on the adventures of the dwarf mage in Lazelan's class on multi-casting. He was famous for wielding more than one spell at a time. During the course of his travels, he had been ambushed by a group of trolls and had cast eight spells at once to best them. The amount of power needed to face even one fourteen-foot troll was mind-boggling, but the man had survived the encounter, supposedly still able to cast. But maybe that's where the history books were wrong. Perhaps that's why he had returned home, burnt out from the experience. It might also explain why he had never used any other spells in front of his people. Lazelan decided that Demar's secrets were his to keep or tell, and so he only responded with a reassurance that he was not a Carrier, nor had he ever studied to be one.

Now there was only one thing left to do as they waited to meet the legendary dwarf. Lazelan walked over to one of the glassy smooth walls, and cast a scrying spell to find Aylan. Surprisingly, it found her in a room that he knew very well. She and the king were standing side-by-side amid his old shelves of potions, pastes, and pills, in what used to be his work room when he had been the former king's mage.

"What kind of magic is this?" Odal breathed reverently, as he watched the swirls of blue on the wall shimmer and show him an image from worlds away.

"Oh, that's nothing," Wolfbane replied, and Lazelan was sure that he heard a note of pride in his companion's voice. "Meet Queen Aylan, and King Oslan the Brave, of Endalwynndale."

Odal gasped, and bowed low in a manner that Lazelan had never seen before. The dwarf made a motion as if grabbing a weapon at his side, and lowered himself to one knee, with his imaginary-weapon-holding-fist hovering about six inches above the ground. "My hammer is your tool, my axe, your blade, and my will, yours to command." he intoned while making eye contact with the king.

Although they could not hear him, they watched as Oslan drew the real sword at his side, regarded it, and laid the blade flat across his empty hand. As he brought the weapon toward his chest as if to accept it, his lips started to move.

"What's he saying?" Wolfbane demanded impatiently to his friend. Lazelan had seen this done a few times when dwarves had come to speak to

King Eurilas, the former ruler that the mage had previously served. He quickly went through Oslan's side of the ritual, speaking the words as the king's lips mouthed them.

"My hammer is skilled, my blade is fierce, and my will is for peace."

A momentary look of panic crossed Aylan's face as her eyes shifted back and forth between her husband and the dwarf. She had obviously never been taught this ritual, and didn't know what to do. In the end, she managed a shallow yet elegant curtsey, and a regally gracious nod of the head. It seemed to be enough for Odal, because he nodded back to her and rose to his feet.

Lazelan smiled at his old pupil, and cast another spell necessary for hearing what she had to say. He pushed his magic farther and farther, to span the distance between them. Maintaining all four tendrils of power drew from his energy source, but he was in no danger of depleting his pool. He had been casting for so long now, and with such skill, that he was quite powerful indeed. This was nothing, although for a new mage, it would be enough to dry up their resources quickly and end their magic using forever.

He bowed and began to make a formal welcome to the royal couple of his own, when he was interrupted by the bang of the door as it was thrown open and it struck the wall. Sasha and Aylan's lady-in-waiting flew into the room, untidy and panting, and screaming like one being tortured for them not to start scrying.

Chapter 28
○ Re-tiring ○

As the words left her lips between gasping breaths, Sasha took in the room. Oslan's startled expression fell and changed to one of worry, while Lazelan's eyes seemed to focus right on her, his brows furrowing in concern. Aylan turned away from the mirror, but Lazelan's image never wavered.

"But we are already speaking with one another," Aylan objected. Her voice sounded unsure as she indicated the four-foot high looking-glass balanced on the wall.

Sasha waved weakly at Lazelan, using only the tips of her fingers, before seeing Wolfbane. The gnome appeared to be trying to elbow the mage out of the way, but as the taller man held his ground, Wolfbane elected to just step in front of his friend to put himself in the foreground.

"Your majesties, hello." he bowed hastily, and then focussed his attention on Sasha. "Even more radiant than the painfully bright fireball behind me, you are a sight for very sore eyes." he told her earnestly with a flowery bow to rival the bards of the court.

Sasha felt her cheeks getting hot as she began to blush from his attentions. She didn't miss the knowing look that Oslan gave Aylan, and the queen's telling smile that was beamed at him in reply.

Only moments after Wolfbane had spoken, Aylan's hand flew to the side of her rounded belly, and the gnome let out a yelp.

"It's happening again!" he warned as his body lifted and his feet came off the floor, pedaling in mid-air as if making contact with the stone would once again ground him.

Sasha hadn't noticed the broad-chested dwarf in the room until he stepped away from the gnome, his thick hands flying up in aversion.

Sasha knew that the queen was already drained from the last time the baby had used her magic, so she suspected what was coming next, and ran to the queen as her friend's knees began to sag.

"Catch her!" Lazelan ordered the king, who looked bewildered, but moved without hesitation. He folded Aylan's considerable form into his arms before she fell in earnest, and lowered her gently to one of the stools that surrounded the work table.

"What is happening?" the dwarf demanded, looking like a squeamish housewife that was ready to jump up onto a chair at the sight of a mouse.

"The baby must have heard Wolfbane's voice," Lazelan informed him. "It seems to like him. It seems to have developed the ability to draw on Queen Aylan's magic, and use any spell that she has since its awareness has grown. It thinks that this is a game."

Oslan looked positively horrified, and shifted his gaze from his wife to the seer to the lady-in-waiting for confirmation. "Is this true?"

"Yes," Sasha confirmed, "that's why we were trying to stop her from scrying. The child hadn't been privy to that one yet, and now it obviously has the power to use her magic long-range. We're afraid that it's going to burn her out, or even kill her if it uses up all of her energy."

"Aylan," he beseeched her, "drop the spell!"

"Unless I miss my guess," Lazelan interjected, "she is currently casting at least three, and all stretch across the kingdom. The danger that we have found is that she has no control over what the baby is doing. Even if she stopped scrying and listening, Wolfbane would likely still float around over here until the baby's playfulness was satisfied."

Aylan braced her arm on the table, and told Oslan, "I meant to let you know the moment that you returned, but your news for Lazelan was so important. We still need to tell him."

Oslan began to explain, "A mermaid came to me when we were hunting near Elbon-"

"Mermaid?" Wolfbane interrupted sceptically. "A real one? I don't think they actually exist. This story is already sounding pretty *fishy* to me."

The gnome's comment triggered something in Sasha's memory. Her mind flicked back through the array of images that had come to her while she had been in her last trance. The woman with the king, the beautiful one with floating hair, that's who it must have been. She felt a little uncomfortable as she remembered the scene, with Oslan in the woman's arms, and their lips almost touching. The seer looked to the ground, embarrassed, but no longer blushing. Then she remembered that the vixen had been trying to hold the king down while his oxygen escaped him. She regarded the king, here in one piece, and was glad that he had survived, because if anything untoward had happened between him and fish-lips, Aylan would want to take care of him herself.

The queen let out a quiet moan and leaned more heavily on the table. "Talk fast," she urged Oslan. The king looked up to Lazelan for some help, some information, anything, and the mage just reiterated what Aylan had already ordered.

"Talk fast," he repeated. Then he tapped Wolfbane on the shoulder with two fingers "There's no time. Let them finish."

Oslan seemed shaken, but went on quickly. "She told me that the Carriers of Brightness have been overseeing the protection of the Almatraek Bright. They keep moving it from one place to the next if they feel that its secret location is close to being discovered.

"So that's why the Carrier has come." Odal intoned from the background.

"A Carrier has arrived already?" Wolfbane asked, seriously this time.

"Yes, this morning. Nalvo is one of the few dwarves that believe all that poppycock about some mystical man showing up to lead people into the light. When Nalvo heard that you had cast magic outside the mountain doors, he assumed that you were from the order too, and raced there to welcome you and assure himself that this time the Carrier's attention wouldn't be snatched up by someone else like it did with this Maewyn Azemar."

Sasha watched as all the colour seemed to drain from Lazelan's face.

"Lazelan, what is it?" Sasha asked, concerned.

"I fear that this quest is already at an end," he told them earnestly. "I have studied this mage; he is both cunning and has a blind faith in his beliefs. I don't think that I can best him if it comes down to a duel, and if he thinks that we are trying to steal the book, no matter how much we know that we need it, he will outright kill us both, and anyone else that might help us. He is a fanatic that believes that anyone who doesn't walk in the brightness, runs with the dark."

"The mermaid suggested that your only hope would be to try to find this book before he does, and get as far from the mountain as quickly as you can." Oslan admitted.

"Can't you merely tell him why you need the book?" Odal piped up.

"It won't work," Oslan insisted, "apparently the only soul on the planet that he'd hand it over to is *he who brightens the way*, from the ancient prophecy."

"Then we better hurry," Wolfbane agreed.

Aylan's head had been slowly nodding closer to the table top. Now her forehead rested on the arm that was holding onto the table. As Sasha was listening to the gnome speak, the image that the mirror showed them began to fade, swirl, and re-solidify. Aylan let out a weak grunt of exertion.

"Lazelan, what can we do for her?" Oslan pleaded.

"The only thing that worked before," Sasha shared, "was when we used a potion that put both her and the baby to sleep."

"Then grab some, let's get it into her!" Oslan ordered. He raced to the shelves, and started lifting and replacing each bottle as he frantically read through their labels.

"She's used it all already," Millie told him, her voice heavy with regret.

"Well what else can we do? Can we make more?"

Lazelan shook his head sadly, "She could make some, but it takes over a week to cure."

"I had a vision this afternoon, maybe it can help." Sasha told them hopefully, "There is a boy, one that my handmaid is always spending time with. I saw him give the queen a basket. I think she fainted when he tried to hand it to her. Maybe we can give her something that will make her faint instead of fall asleep?"

Lazelan's eyebrows shot up as if he had just made a realization. "Aylan, you can make up more packets like those that you used to drain Zaltreous' power when he was being held prisoner in the tower." As the mage spoke, the picture faded from the mirror's surface and was replaced by a reflection of the laboratory, but Lazelan got one last word in before the sound faded completely. "You must cast energy draw to save yourself while the child continues to use your magic. It might be the only way." His voice sounded as if it was coming down a long hallway now, and even took on an echoing quality before the sound was cut off. The queen gasped when it did.

"Energy draw, of course, you have to!" Oslan told Aylan fervently. She shook her head weakly, letting her forehead roll from side to side across her forearm.

"I won't put you in danger like that. You're the ruler of this kingdom, the people need you."

Millie rushed to the queen's side. "You can use me, Your Majesty."

The queen smiled at her lady-in-waiting. "Thank you, Millie, but I still cannot."

"Why not?" Oslan demanded hotly. "By the shields of the army of Ormond, Aylan, you could die! Cast the blooming spell!" His fist slammed into the table top as if to punctuate the dread welling up in his gullet.

She smiled fondly at him. "Oslan, this is bigger than just me. If I cast that spell, the baby..." she let her voice trail off, and her glazed eyes blinked far too slowly. Her face had taken on a too pale, ashy grey sheen to it, and dark shadows were beginning to form under her eyes. She looked like a person suffering from a severe flu.

Sasha went to kneel in front of her friend. "Aylan, I think you should take the chance. If Oslan's knights can get you the ingredients that you need for your packets, it won't matter if the baby learns the spell, because it won't be able to cast it.

Draw more energy from us, and hopefully that will give you the stamina you need to last until the packets are ready."

Finally, the queen acquiesced. She closed her eyes and as she said the words, her voice got softer until it came out in a lagging whisper that could barely be heard.

"Tarax tritae nula kraku, tigo Ey tayt tiris." *Two points of power, lend me your strength.*

Immediately, Sasha felt some invisible force reach into her and she could feel her own energy level drop slightly. Meanwhile, Aylan's eyes flashed open.

"Oslan," the queen said in a much more steady voice, "you need to get me the things that I require for those packets. Here is a list." She grabbed a piece of stray parchment off the work table, dipped her quill in her inkpot, and began to jot down one plant after another. Finally, she poured some sand on the words to dry them, and shook the paper to let the sand fall back into the bowl where she kept it.

Sasha's vigour was beginning to wane. She sat to conserve energy, and noticed that Millie had already begun to lean against the door.

"Oslan, I would suggest that you get your fastest riders, and someone who is familiar with some of those herbs." Sasha advised. "If the baby is able to do to other people what the spell is doing to us right now, you should try to get back as fast as humanly possible. We know that the baby can send Aylan's magic across the kingdom, and I fear that the baby has a fascination with Wolfbane. I believe that he might be the most likely target." A pit of dread had turned into a hard knot in her stomach. She realized that her hands where clasped together nervously in front of her md-section, and she deliberately released them. She inconspicuously wiggled her fingers to try to dry the nervous sweat that had sprung up on her palms.

"I have no way of knowing who the spell might be targeting if I'm not the one casting it." Aylan concurred. "Hopefully the baby won't try to reach Wolfbane and randomly hit another ruler out there with the spell instead."

"That could become a dire situation." Oslan admitted. "I will leave immediately."

"This isn't too bad," Millie told them, "It's just making me a little tired. It wouldn't really hurt them if it did."

Sasha was getting so frustrated. It was hard to catch someone up when they were out of the loop. She fought to keep her tone as that of one adult speaking with another, so she didn't speak down to the maid like she might an imbecile or a child. "But if the baby didn't call off the spell, it could kill the target." Sasha reminded her.

"Any mage knows that casting on a ruler would be like striking them," Aylan remarked. "If they found out the spell came from me, they could call for my head. Even if it was only a member of the nobility, they might rally our subjects into a revolt."

This was worse than Sasha had thought. She had only been thinking of Aylan's safety, she hadn't considered that it might affect the whole kingdom. She was glad that she was already sitting down.

"To make matters worse," Oslan added, always considering the royal implications, "if the baby did manage to even touch another king or queen with any spell, it could end our kingdom's generations of peace, as it would be construed as an act of war."

Chapter 29
O Under-Mined O

The king's statement about war rang out in the otherwise silenced sapphire room. Lazelan had guessed that Aylan had been unable to maintain the two spells under her control when the other group had stopped watching the mirror. His suspicions were confirmed when they quit reacting to the words spoken on this side of the kingdom. Lazelan had continued his scrying to see if they could come up with any other solutions to his former pupil's problem. From what he'd seen, they hadn't.

A lump formed in his throat at the thought of losing her. He had worked closely with Aylan since she had been a young and rather awkward girl. She had had a flare for herbology though, and had excelled in the use of magic. He had taught her almost everything he knew about being a mage, and she had been a natural.

Before that, he had worked for Oslan's father, King Eurilas, and he knew how important the family's legacy of peace was. He couldn't let Endalwynndale end in war, even if he had to undertake the impossible task of facing Maewyn Azemar to do it.

He looked over at the gnome who was still bobbing quite comfortably in the air. He had drawn his dagger, and was using the tip of it to clean the dirt out from under his nails. The knife was not suited for the task. It was more like an inelegantly held short sword for someone of Wolfbane's stature. They weren't going to stand a chance.

On the shimmering stone wall, Lazelan watched as King Oslan kissed Aylan deeply on the forehead and raced from the laboratory. Sasha and Millie each took one of the queen's arms over their shoulders, and the three of them hobbled out of the room, supporting each other like three squires that had been injured in their first tournament.

Lazelan let the image on the wall fade and allowed his two far-reaching spells to end. Without forcibly pulling the energy from his core to continue making his incantations work, the tendrils of power raced back through him to the pool of energy where it always stayed at rest. The endeavour always left him feeling a bit drained and hollow afterwards. It was hard to have the power of magic run through you, filling you with awareness and life, and then have it just be gone. That empty sensation would pass quickly enough though.

Wolfbane had sheathed his dagger and was staring at the spot on the wall where the image had faded. Then with a cry, the floating gnome suddenly fell to the ground. With a groan, he picked himself up and rubbed his bruised tailbone. He didn't often sound alarmed, but now when he spoke, there was no question that that's what he was feeling.

"Lazelan, they didn't look so good at the end there."

"I know," the mage answered quietly.

"I'm not sure that they're going to make it. I mean, it's going to take a while for the king to collect those things."

"My thoughts exactly." Lazelan said dourly.

"What will happen to Sasha and the other one, if the queen doesn't stop?" Wolfbane's words were enveloped in concern now.

"Assuming that the queen is able to drop the spell by her own free will, she would do so before any permanent damage befell the others. Aylan is made of an admirable mettle. She would allow herself to lose her magic before she would harm her friends." He explained soothingly. "However, if the baby takes over, or reaches out again for the same target, I fear that it will be the end for all of them."

"Lazelan, we have to get the Almatraek Bright, surely there's something inside it that can save them." Wolfbane stated.

"I was thinking the same thing," Lazelan admitted, "but time is short, and I'll need the opportunity to look through the pages for something that could help."

"How are we going to go about finding it, and before the Carrier of Brightness nabs it first?"

"I'll help you," Odal said simply. Lazelan jumped, having almost completely forgotten about the dwarven clan chief standing in the corner.

"You will?" Wolfbane and Lazelan asked in unison.

"Of course," the dwarf replied as if there was no question as to why he wouldn't. He stroked his beard sagely as he spoke. "The way I see it, our queen needs our help. If that book contains something that could save her, then keeping it hidden on purpose should be considered an act of treason."

Lazelan had never given any thought to the hierarchy of the people involved, it hadn't even occurred to him. When dealing with ancient orders, the members seemed to assume that it superseded any ruler and so were above the law. But now that the idea had been spoken aloud, Lazelan agreed. The men that made up the Carriers of Brightness were just as much members of the kingdom as he was. They ate the food that its farmers produced, and lived in a dwelling within its borders. The rules had to apply to them too.

Lazelan thought of leaving the nice warm room that he had created, and shook once as a shiver ran though him. He grabbed his burgundy cloak off the bed and did up the clasp at the throat. The velvet hung heavily on his shoulders. As soon as Lazelan raised its deep hood and the trim's blazing suns came together in the front, he warmed noticeably. He allowed the hovering fireball to wink out, and though a torch still burned on the wall, it seemed as though they were plunged into darkness. Lazelan's eyes once again tried to adjust to the severe dimness of the stunning cave.

"We need to find a way to distract or delay the Carrier." Wolfbane suggested.

"That should be fairly easy," Odal smiled. He opened the door to the room, and spoke excitedly to the nearest passing dwarf. Then, to Wolfbane and Lazelan, he said, "Let's go."

"What did you tell them?" Wolfbane asked.

"I told her to let Nalvo know that the Carrier had time to answer his questions now," the dwarf let them in on his trick. "Nalvo will scurry over there and will talk to him for hours."

"Can you be sure?" Lazelan inquired.

"I nearly died today because Nalvo was so star struck with the man that his incessant prattling prevented my rescue until it was almost too late," the dwarf enlightened them as they headed out the door.

Lazelan thought that he was starting to get a good idea of the type of man that Nalvo was. He hoped that the dwarf with the message would reach him before they did.

Odal led them through the blue halls, checking the rune markings at each place that the corridors intersected. He was studying the dwarven writing at one such place when the echoes of footsteps came up the hall from a distance to the side.

"Quickly," Odal instructed, "get back in the tunnel, and hide against the wall. I'll draw his attention away. It's not every day that we dwarves get to see a real human or gnome, and I don't want you to be remembered or detained."

Lazelan and Wolfbane complied, pressing their backs up against the wall and trying their best to stand stone still. Any movement at the most inopportune time would draw the eye of the passer by.

It was only a few seconds later that Lazelan became aware of a sensation that made him begin to perspire and fill him with dread. He could feel an uneasy tickle way in the back of his nose. *I'm going to sneeze!* he lamented. The footsteps drew closer, echoing each thud and scrape of the dwarf's leather-soled boots. The irritated sensation in Lazelan's nasal passage grew insistent. There was a light *shif, shif,* sound as the oncoming dwarf's leather robe rubbed against his sleeves as he swung his arms with each step. It was hardly enough to cover the sound of the impending nasal explosion, though. Lazelan screwed his eyes shut, as his breath began to do that familiar leading-up-to-the-sneeze hitching.

"Press your tongue to the back of your upper front teeth!" Wolfbane hissed, timing his words with the steps of the dwarf that was now only a couple of seconds away. Lazelan didn't know if the dwarf had heard, but his movements never faltered. The mage did as the gnome had suggested, thinking *it's too late, what's that going to do?* But as he inhaled deeply in preparation for the sneeze, the pressure of his tongue on the back of his teeth worked! For some miracle of a reason, the urge crept away and he was able to silently let his breath back out slowly.

The footsteps sounded as if they were right on top of the small party now, and Odal crossed the hall away from them and greeted the other dwarf briefly, so that his head would be turned away from the tunnel where the mage and gnome were hiding.

"Good digging to you," Odal intoned in a practiced voice.

The other dwarf seemed to take in Odal's outfit, and the fact that his heavy coat was trimmed in brown and gold instead of the blue that it should have been in this set of tunnels, but he still returned what Lazelan assumed was the standard response.

"And a cartload to you." the rather deep and gruff voice answered as the other dwarf continued on his way without pausing in his course.

Lazelan had been a scholar all his life, and had never had to be very stealthy before. His heart was pounding from almost getting caught. Action didn't bother him; he could battle a five headed dragon with magic and not think twice about it. What he didn't want to have to deal with was being delayed while such a talented mage and wonderful person lost her abilities or died. Being discovered would mean having to explain why they were attempting to make off with a tome that was hundreds of years old, and he didn't fancy having to plead with a fanatic Carrier, who was the book's self-appointed guardian. First, he was going to have to make it to Demar, and state their case with him. Then maybe he'd show them where the book was.

"How far is it until we can get to Demar?" the mage asked once they had crossed into the new tunnel and had almost made it to the brightening entrance to the ball room where all of the clan's tunnels converged.

"I'm not taking you to see Demar," Odal told the mage without slowing, "I know where the Almatraek Bright is hidden. I'm going to take you straight to the book."

Lazelan was shocked at their good fortune, there may actually be hope! He felt like skipping or running ahead, but he had to remind himself that both of the men he was travelling with had a much shorter stride. He kept going at the speed that the dwarf had set, and clasped his hands in front of him in joy. They were on their way to the book! But his feeling of elation was hampered by fear as Wolfbane added, "I just hope that the Carrier hasn't already been led there as well."

Chapter 30
O Hide Out O

When Oslan bolted from the laboratory, leaving his suffering wife behind, he took the stairs back down the hallway two at a time. His heart was in anguish as the heels of his boots pounded on the flagstones, and he willed himself to move faster. He had never sped through that secret passage so fast in his life, and he was stricken when he found that he had to pull up short before bursting out from behind the tapestry to the war room. There were voices, low pitched and incredulous.

"Ladies don't just disappear, where did they go?" the first voice asked. Oslan recognized it immediately. It belonged to a gruff knight named Reginald that had been away in the port town patrolling the docks and checking the cargo of the boats that came and went. He had only just returned with a few other men after having been stationed there for years. The king had put them on a rotation of posts throughout the castle so they could get used to the schedule of the keep, and the faces of those that lived here.

Oslan didn't know how he was going to think his way around this one. But he was burning inside to yell *come on!* at them. *Move along, get out, I need to go!* he willed them urgently. He had to get to the woods, and the sooner the better. Aylan was depending on him. He would have been shifting his weight and bouncing from foot to foot in impatience, but he forced himself to stand stalk still in case any movement would cause a sound. He tried to think of a way of explaining his departure from a room that the knights had now seen to be empty. Then an opportunity presented itself.

"Perhaps they left while you ran to see about those sphinxes." a second voice answered. "If that was the case, you have nothing to fear, you were under Osmond's orders."

"Are you daft? You were still here. That was a waste of my time anyway," the other said sullenly, "We never got to see any action at all. The cats didn't even attack at the castle."

Sir Reginald was used to a rougher sort of encounter on the docks that teamed with sailors that had been into the rum. Perhaps he needed some excitement. Oslan was prepared to give him some.

When he heard the door to the war room bang shut and the voices of the guards slowly fade, Oslan wasted no time in leaving the passageway. By now his breath had slowed, and he fought to make himself keep to a mere walking gait. Leaving the war room, he passed through the armoury, grabbed his legendary sword, Skirdkhen, from its mount on the wall, and slowly opened the door to the hallway.

Both knights jumped as the door moved, and Oslan quite satisfactorily found himself at spear-point for a mere second before the guards realized who he was. They hastily dropped their weapons and saluted him immediately. Both had gone white as a ghost.

"Your Majesty, how?" The first guard asked, seemingly mystified.

Oslan let one corner of his mouth turn up in a smile. "We never left, gentlemen. My wife makes invisibility pills, which are quite remarkable." Although his statements were meant to be misleading, both were technically true. Hopefully if he could get them to believe this story, then they wouldn't spend any time poking around the room, looking for another way out.

"Invisible?" Sir Reginald protested, "But that's impossible, Your Grace."

"I can assure you, that when magic is involved, you should be prepared to expect almost anything." the king said wryly. Then to prove his point, he continued quickly, "Sir Reginald, you sounded very disappointed a moment ago when you were lamenting about the lack of action in relation to the sphinxes that flew by. No doubt you'll get to see them again on their way back to the Embralic Desert."

Both guards gaped at him. *Excellent,* he mused. *My ruse seems to have worked.*

"Now, Sir Reginald, if you wouldn't mind accompanying me, I will be heading into the king's forest. There are two others that I must collect. Meet me near the postern gates as quickly as possible. We will be going on horseback, so get the stable boy to prepare four horses."

With that, Reginald threw his spear to the other guard, gave him the kingdom's salute, and raced away with the king.

Chapter 31
O Cold Feet O

Odal had led the tall gangly mage and the much shorter gnome into the tunnel marked by his own clan's gemstones. The walls shone with the tigers-eye's bands of black and gold. The gold seemed almost like liquid as the yellow torchlight glinted off the flecks in the rock. All this was almost lost on Odal though, who had lived within these halls his whole life. To him, they were common place, just the plain old corridors that he had grown up in. They stopped briefly at a set of rooms. They were not quite as fancy as the ones that the chief of the sapphire clan possessed, but they were not plain. Odal freed a battle axe from a mount on the wall, and strapped it to his back with a thick criss-crossing leather harness. As they returned to the hallways and progressed on their way, Odal hoped that it wouldn't come to using it.

Odal didn't bother telling either of the sun soakers just how lucky they had been that Nalvo had deserted them when he had. If he had been privy to their little conversation with the king and queen, then the blond dwarf may have done all in his power to prevent the gnome and the human from ever reaching the Almatraek Bright.

The chief of the sapphire clan wasn't evil; he just always had his own self interests in the forefront of his mind. He fully believed in the prophecy, no matter how ludicrous it sounded to most of the other dwarves. Although the dwarven cities were technically under the kingdom's rule, the queen was almost a world away. Meanwhile, the Carrier of Brightness was right here where Nalvo could act on his behalf and maybe be written into their teachings as a great hero and protector of the book.

Odal quickened his pace. His breath was coming in huffs and puffs now, especially now that he was carrying the weight of the heavy weapon. He had been very fit in his mining days, although being in shape for a dwarf meant being as solid, as wide, and as heavy as a mason's stone wall. However, since he had become clan chief, sadly, Odal had filled out a bit more in the middle, and the sleeves around his biceps seemed to have become a little loose without the constant exercise of swinging an axe. With all of this brisk walking, he was beginning to feel his extra girth.

Being clan chief might have ruined his figure, but it had afforded him access to information that most Dwarves weren't privy to. When the position had been passed to him, he had been sequestered in a vault for almost a week. Inside, the only furniture had been a large table with an elaborate candelabrum, and a single chair. There were no real walls. Instead, the perimeter had been hollowed out in horizontal rows to create shelves that surrounded the entire space. Each of the shelves contained massive books as thick as his arm, or ancient scrolls made of long sections of parchment. These were the histories of his people, ledgers tallying the wealth of the dwarves, the names and lineage of everyone that had ever lived within the mountain, the teachings of the prophecy and other legends, and of course, the Almatraek Bright.

The stone room was located in the old part of the tunnel system that had been built by their ancestors. Down in the bowels of the mountain, the mine shafts had been roughly hewn, and no time had been taken to make them presentable.

These were the tunnels that Odal led Lazelan and Wolfbane to. There was no sparkle or shine left on the walls, as all of the veins of gems had been exhausted. This meant that the torchlight had nothing to reflect off of, so the light that the fire offered only allowed them to see a few feet ahead or behind them. It was creepy and disconcerting even to the dwarf that had worked in mineshafts quite like this one for the better part of his adult life. Even though there was no one else down here, the darkened tunnel gave the impression that someone or something could jump out at them at any moment.

Odal felt the mage and the gnome draw nearer to him, presumably to be able to see farther down the tunnel. It didn't help that every time they passed a ventilation shaft, the flow of air would make the torch dance and sometimes the flame would start to gutter. Odal prayed that the fire wouldn't go out.

The group criss-crossed through many intersecting shafts, sometimes turning right at one corner, and then left a minute later at the next. Odal sometimes paused briefly, but never hesitated. He had only been to this level a couple of times and couldn't have possibly memorized the way, but the tunnels were clearly marked. The corridors down here were even more mazelike than the more organized ones above. Here they had to deal with underground springs, and sadly, some shafts had been barred due to cave-ins or other mishaps that had made them unsafe or unfit to travel through.

Even though Odal was reading the dwarven runes, it still felt like they were doubling back sometimes. It made him impatient, but he knew that they were getting there the in the only way that they could. He strained to listen for voices as they closed in on the final tunnel. Wolfbane's coin purses and scabbards hanging from his belt made an awful clamour as he moved, and Odal had to stop them often so they could listen ahead. He didn't want any surprises down here. All there was to hear was the faint clanging and clanking of picks on rock resonating through the stone from miners working away on some level above. Finally, as they were walking, the clinking of the gnome's gait stopped, and Odal had to look back to see if they had lost him. As it turned out, Wolfbane had just separated his pouches and had tied them higher so they would no longer swing to and fro to collide with one another or the chain mail that he wore under his breastplate. Odal silently breathed a sigh of relief as they carried on.

The rhythmic sound of water intermittently dripping into a pool joined the sound of the distant picks. As they proceeded up the corridor, the sound grew louder by degrees, echoing down the hall as if to gauge their progress by its volume. Then Odal heard a brief splashing up ahead, accompanied by a curse in a familiar voice, and the much closer sound of metal being drawn across leather. He turned to speak to the sun soakers, but to their credit, they must have heard it, too. Wolfbane was standing with his short-sword of a dagger drawn. The mage's lips were moving silently and his brows were furrowed, giving his face the same look of concentration as a small dwarf learning his runes.

"Nalvo is here." Odal warned in a voice that was barely a whisper. "He is heading to the same vault that we are; there isn't much else down here. Why, and with whom though, I can't tell you for certain."

They continued along the tunnel warily, not speaking. Odal handed the torch to the mage. He hoped to get some more distance out of the small amount of light if the fire were held higher. It worked, but only marginally. He wondered how they were going to traverse the shallow pool of water themselves without tipping off whoever else was ahead. Odal remembered the spot well, because the first time that he had been led down here, he had been warned to remove his boots to avoid having to sit in the vault for hours with cold wet feet.

Sooner than he would have liked, the surface of the water came into view as it reflected the glow of their torch, and beyond it, a yellow beam of light shone on what appeared to be a dead end. The mage whispered something in a language that the dwarf didn't understand, "Laeat nae in etallil." *Surround us in silence."* Then the mage looked at Odal, pointed at the water, and held his hand level by his ankle, then his shin, then his knee, then his waist.

It was obvious that the mage wanted to know about the depth of the pool, but the dwarf didn't know why the gangly man hadn't just asked him. Odal's lips moved to warn them, "It's only about knee deep, but ice cold." However, no sound came from the dwarf. His hands clasped his throat in horror. *What did he do to my voice?* the dwarf thought in panic. He moved his fingers across the skin on his throat. His neck felt fine, there was no pain. He tried shouting. The veins and tendons stood out in his effort to yell, which was still producing no sound. He pointed at the mage, and mouthed *Did you do this?*

Lazelan nodded. Odal watched as the mage searched around briefly with his eyes, then stooped to pick up a hefty rock that lay where the wall met the floor. He threw it underhand so that it arced through the air. Odal could tell that it was going to land right in the middle of the pool. *What in all the kingdom was the imbecile thinking? As soon as the rock hits, Nalvo and his band will be upon us, and with the Carrier, none the less. I thought that mages had to have some level of intelligence, but this sun soaker is obviously not the brightest gem in the chest.* He shook his head in denial as the rock reached the apex of the throw and started its downward trajectory. He watched, dumbfounded, without a thing that could be done to stop it.

The dwarf cringed, his eyes squinting as he awaited the condemning impact. The throw had been a great one, and the rock splashed into the water with enough force to create an impressive shower that sprayed the walls on either side of the tunnel. Odal was stunned. The sound of the rock colliding with the water should have carried all the way down the hall in either direction. But it hadn't made a sound. He realized then that although he could still hear the miners picking away at the rock tunnels above, the immediate sound of the water dripping into the pool here had ceased. The mage had shrouded their entire area in complete and utter silence. His eyes opened wide in amazement. *That sun soaker just might be the sharpest peak on the mountain!*

Odal wasted no more time. He pointed to the water, and then showed them how deep it would be with his hand against his own leg. He stooped briefly to remove his boots, and held them up for the others to see so they would know to follow suit. Then, he stepped into the frigid water and sucked in his breath. He would have squealed from the shock of the cold temperature if he could have made any sound. If his feet had just gone numb, it would have been a blessing. But the experience was almost painful as the frigidity of the pool caused his feet to feel like pins and needles were all jabbing at him at once. Not to mention that as he traversed the obstacle, leftover rocks jabbed up at the bottoms of his tender insteps. He gingerly picked his way to the other side. Finally, once he was across, he gave each foot a shake, and immediately pulled on his woolen socks and stout boots. Warmth began to circulate back into his feet as the other two made the trek through the water. Under any other circumstances, the grimaces on their faces might have been considered comical. As it was though, the vault was now in sight. The stone door stood at the dead end, closed and always locked by magic. There were runes etched across its surface that were bathed in the light of two torches that hung to either side of it. A trail of three sets of soggy footprints led to the vault. The last footprint disappeared half way under the door, meaning that Nalvo, the Carrier, and whoever else had accompanied them, were already inside.

Chapter 32
O Cloaked in Darkness O

Oslan's chestnut steed flicked his mane and stomped at the ground impatiently as the king held him still to wait for the last of his knights. Archer, the king's large peregrine falcon, sat contentedly on Oslan's thickly gloved hand. The bluish-black feathers covering her head, wings, and back looked like a majestic cape that stood out opposite her white throat and brown body. The king glanced at Sir Carn and Sir Reginald, who already sat side by side on their mounts, and looked almost like opposites.

Carn would be celebrating his thirty-seventh birthday in a month, but the small crow's feet beside his icy blue eyes were the only hint to his age. His broad shoulders, muscular build, clean-shaven square jaw, and wide forehead made him a man that many ladies had fawned over. His thick blond hair gleamed in the sun as the tips of his wavy locks brushed the shoulders of his navy blue tabard.

Reginald on the other hand, had not aged well. He appeared to be at least a decade older, and his black hair was beginning to be streaked with grey. Having been on duty moments before outside the armoury, he wore his full suit of armour, which helped to cover up the extra weight that he was carrying around his middle. His round jaw had sprouted a shadow of stubble that was also flecked with grey, making the cleft in his pointy chin almost unnoticeable.

Carn seemed only half dressed in his less cumbersome hauberk and tabard compared to the other knight. But he still managed to sit straighter in the saddle and looked slightly more formidable than Sir Reginald, who appeared as though he were slouching even when he wasn't.

"Who is this *boy* we wait for?" Reginald whispered to Carn disdainfully.

"His Royal Majesty has requested that one of his archers join us." Carn replied calmly. "It is always beneficial to have someone along that can shoot at a distance, especially when we go in search of things for the queen. It wouldn't do to get into a skirmish and trample a precious herb or root plant that could help her cure one of her subjects."

Carn's lecture was interrupted as Thorn came running, his bow and quiver hanging off of one shoulder, and a large wicker basket clutched in one hand. The teen looked as though he had thrown on his gear in a hurry, as his short dark brown hair was mussed, and his tabard was askew where his belt synched it and his mail to his thin waist.

"I'm sorry, Os-" Thorn, who had grown up with the king, and often spoke with him rather informally, cut off in mid-sentence as he took in the old knight that would be part of their party. Without skipping a beat, he finished formally, "Your Majesty, I'm here." He wasted no time, and mounted up on the dappled grey and white horse the stable boy held for him.

"We have no time to spare. Queen Aylan is dying," Oslan told them. He took a deep breath to steady a voice that was on the verge of cracking in grief. The shock registering in his knights' eyes was plain. "We must go into the king's forest past the third grove of trees, that's where she said to start looking for the herbs she needs to save herself."

"Then why aren't we going, man, don't you love your wife? Why do we sit here waiting?" Sir Reginald asked hotly as his steed started to skitter sideways.

The stress of the thought of losing Aylan had been eating at Oslan the whole time as he had anxiously awaited Thorn, who was the best at spotting the herbs that his wife often used. He was necessary to their success, as he often took on the detail of accompanying her into the woods. It had taken every ounce of conviction Oslan had had to keep up the appearance of calm poise as he waited for his friend to show. Outrage overcame him with every insulting word that Reginald flung at him. The king's teeth gritted together to stifle the rebuke that instantly rose to his lips. If he had been any less of a man, Oslan would have punched the buffoon. As it was, the king heard the faint sound of Carn's leather glove tighten on his reins, and was relieved that it hadn't been just him that had had the impulse. Oslan's father had taught him from a young age that harsh words spoken in anger from a ruler had been the cause of everything from beheadings to full scale wars, and some things couldn't be taken back once spoken. Oslan forced himself to breathe deeply and count to ten before he had responded, as his father had taught him.

Thorn however, had never had such training. The teen's usual unremarkable voice took on the resonating tones that he used when performing. His voice smoothly carried for everyone to hear. "There is no love deeper than that that exists between the king and the queen of Endalwynndale!" Thorn declared, "The very bond between them saved our entire kingdom not yet a year past." He lowered his voice without losing any of the impressive weight that it carried, "The insult you hurl at the king is tantamount to treason, and I would put you down right here, if it weren't for the fact that you wear the fire as my brother in arms!"

Reginald's horse shied away from the group a couple more steps. The old knight's face reddened as he finally realized what he had said and to whom the comment had been made. He gave a hasty apology, looking back and forth between the king, and Thorn, whose free hand had flown to the sword hilt that hung from his belt.

Oslan held up his hand to stop his friend, and said "Galloping into the forest, and having our horses trod on things the queen means us to retrieve will not help us, nor her. Going not knowing what we seek first could mean us having to waste time, which would also be detrimental. I will give you each a couple of ingredients that we seek now, and by splitting up, it should save us a great amount of time." He read off the list, and found that Thorn could describe the plants quite well. They would be able to recognize all they needed, except for one that the boy hadn't known. The king would worry about that when they had the rest. By the brightness, something always seemed to show them the way when they most needed guidance. He hoped that this time would be no different.

*   *   *

Sasha had been laying on the cold flagstone floor of the war room for almost a full minute before Millie dropped down beside her. The seer had tried to escape through the war room with the queen as her life force had been leeched away. She had helped Aylan as far as she could, before Sasha had simply lacked the strength to stand. Her knees had buckled, and she had gone down hard, her weakened arms hadn't had the ability to stop her cheek from cracking off the floor, and the sticky heat coming from the spot on her face told her that she had endured the injury of a scrape at the very least. She groaned. She was fighting to hold onto consciousness, but it was a battle that she was losing. Each time she closed her eyes, a vision of a golden fiery torch pendant filled her mind. She didn't know what it meant. She only knew that the pull that was dragging her energy from her was almost through. She didn't have any more to give.

"Sasha, wake up! I'll get help! I'll call the guard and just tell them that one of my potions made you ill."

Sasha's eyes opened lazily once again. The queen's radiant face swam into view as her coherence solidified. "No, you mustn't," the seer begged her, "If you make a claim such as that, you open yourself to all manner of complaint. The subjects that come to you for help could begin to make up falsehoods about your magic. They could begin to accuse you if things don't go their way. It could lead to a revolt. It is better to appear to remain flawless to them." Her words came out in a breathless muzzy slur. "Tell the guard that we tried to make off with one of your scrolls, and that you had to subdue us."

The queen looked vexed. "Sasha, never!" she shook her head in negation. "You are my most trusted friends. If I made a claim like that, I would have to put you on trial and banish you from the castle as thieves. I would never do that."

Sasha's eyes slid closed again. That golden pendant shimmered into view. There was nothing else, just blackness. Light glinted off the gold chain of a necklace that the pendant must be hanging from. The shadows played across it, the light making the torch's fire seem alive. Sasha could feel herself falling deeper and deeper into her own subconscious. The pull for sleep was enormous, and just too big to fight any longer. The queen was calling her name, but the seer couldn't rise out of the depths of her gift. She felt at piece as she gave over to exhaustion. The queen was summoning the guard, her voice coming from very far away, but it was too late for Sasha now, what could a guard do, anyway?

The faint syphoning of her energy had dwindled to a trickle that Sasha could barely feel. Her emotions had left her, too. She no longer felt the sharp anguish that she had experienced from the realization that was going to die. Her awareness of what was going on around her had gotten dimmer as her lucidity had left her. The feeling of loss had even petered out, and Sasha was left lying on the floor in a void that she couldn't come back from. Her breathing had become shallow and sporadic, and the only thing left was the glimmering image of the golden torch floating in the darkness of her mind. A red light flashed across the surface of the pendant, and was gone again. Then even that was taken from her as the thing that she dreaded rolled across the image, blocking it out by degrees. It kept coming until it had eclipsed the vision completely, and she was aware of no more.

Chapter 33
O Being Picky O

Oslan's band had galloped to the forest at full speed. Once they had reached the forest trails, they had been slowed so as not to have their horses break a leg on an overgrown root, but they had still made good headway. Splitting up, they had found what they sought after quickly enough, though the passage of time still pulled at Oslan like a persistent child. They were almost finished with their list now, as they rejoined each other to deliver the ingredients to the basket Thorn had set down in order to pull up the second last plant that they searched for. All back on their horses now except for the young bard, they gave him words of encouragement as the plant wouldn't budge. Thorn heaved with all his might until with a great earthy sound, the root began to move.

"Ugh!" Carn let out an involuntary gasp of revulsion and covered his nose with the crook of his elbow as the teen pulled the root free from the ground. It hadn't smelled bad while it was growing, but with the red root exposed, it reeked like uncooked rotten meat.

Oslan's felt his last meal threaten to rise in his gorge as the pungent odour hit his nose, and he tried to fight the sensation back down. Even Archer flapped her wings majestically and strained against her jesses, trying to take flight. Oslan took pity on his grand bird, unhooded her, and released her into the sky.

He waved at the root as if trying to shoo it away. "Quickly, wrap it in something!" he ordered, thinking that in doing so, it might at least lessen the offensive aroma. Even the horses were attempting to turn and walk away from it, and they repeatedly snorted as if to clear their nostrils.

But the knights weren't carrying any cloth that could be used, and none of them were about to rip a strip from the tabard he wore that bore their hard earned dragon's fire. Finally, as he sat upon his horse, gagging, Thorn removed his tabard completely and rolled the root up within it.

Oslan found that he was able to breathe the fresh scent of the forest again. "I'll issue you a new tabard. That one, we will burn," he announced indicating the bundle being added to the basket.

"Now we just have to find the woodbine," Carn declared.

"I haven't seen it before," Thorn informed them mournfully.

"She described it as looking something like a honeysuckle," Oslan informed them. Look for a yellow flower on a vine that may be climbing a tree."

They turned the horses down the path that would carry them deeper into the forest, but before they left the grove, a dull *clang*, rung out across the vale as something struck the back of Sir Reginald's armour. The sound was much like a wooden spoon striking a pot.

Oslan watched as Reginald wheeled his horse around in confusion, trying to catch the culprit that should have been standing behind him. There was no one on the path. As soon as the horse stopped moving, another clang followed, this time coming from almost above them.

"This forest is haunted!" Reginald shrieked. The words were no sooner out of his mouth than a loud metallic *ka-chunk*, sounded out as Reginald's breastplate separated from the back and fell loosely off of one shoulder.

The surprised knight yelped out an affronted "Yikes!" and grabbed at the armour to try to hold it closed. The buckle lay unharmed. Someone had worked it open.

A high-pitched miniature tinkling laughter chittered through the glen, passing from one voice to another, but there was no sign of another soul.

"What was that?" Reginald asked, sounding spooked.

Ki-yee! The falcon's cry pierced the air right before she dove out of the sky. Wings tucked back and falling at a blinding speed, she plummeted down, closing in on whatever prey she had spotted. She was heading toward Sir Reginald, and in a streak of brown feathers, she picked something off the horse's back, and pinned it to the ground on the thoroughbred's other side.

The horse had been startled at the sudden feeling of the bird's weight and sharp feet, and had begun to kick and rear. It took off with Sir Reginald crying "Whoa!" and still trying to hold onto his armour.

Oslan knew what would come next with his bird, and as a tiny terrified scream erupted from the thing caught in the predator's talons, the king whistled to call Archer off before she bobbed her sleek head to make the kill. He waved his arms, and reached for a pouch hanging from his belt. She hesitated, and his heart pounded as he hoped fervently that she would choose to listen.

Oslan quickly grabbed a piece of food for Archer from the leather purse, and held it out to her in his thick black leather glove. He repeated the whistle, and she turned her head to him. She took a step in his direction, and in doing so, dragged her prize through the dirt. The wee thing bawled as soil scraped along its side. Oslan whistled again, this time adding the command for her to return with his voice. Archer took another dragging step toward him before flying up to his glove. Once she landed, he rewarded her hunting skills by giving her the meaty morsel he had enticed her with, and managed to get a fairy-sized girl loose from his raptor's grasp.

He looked at the lass, who stood no taller than a goodly sized apple. Her bark-coloured frizzy hair was shoulder length, but stood out in a fluffy halo around her head, except for where the mud had matted it down on one side. Her garments were made from the hide of a small rodent, with fur lining the edges. Her whole left side was covered in a thick coating of dirt where the falcon had dragged her through the forest's moist soil. She tried to brush herself off indignantly as the king set her on the pommel of his saddle and hooded Archer to avoid any further attacks.

Oslan's first encounter with a forest imp had been with a small male the year that Aylan had first moved into the castle to learn magic. The tiny humanoid had snuck around playing tricks on them until Aylan had caught it with magic. This selfsame little man now made an appearance as he dropped out of a tree, landing on Oslan's shoulder. He scampered down the king's arm to reach the female, pulling her into a desperate hug.

"Scritch, is that you?" the king asked. To Oslan's surprise, the miniscule man looked very different from the first time they had met. His formerly dishevelled brown hair was now combed after a fashion, and his clothes were all neatly fastened, with any tears mended by a practiced hand.

The imp finally let the female go and turned to Oslan, the relief plain on his face. The normally obnoxious little man gave the king a rather formal bow. Oslan knew that he wouldn't be able to make out anything that the imp might say, but he figured that if anyone would know what the flower they needed looked like, the imps should. Trying to communicate with him was worth a try.

"Do you know the woodbine plant?" the king asked gently. The imp appeared to be thinking about it, going as far as to scratch his head as he thought. "It has a yellow flower, and the vine may climb up a tree." Oslan added.

The little female started clapping her hands excitedly, and making motions like she was blowing a horn. Scritch took her hands in his and gave her a brief peck on the cheek. Then he pointed in a direction back toward the castle. With Oslan in the lead, and the imps indicating the way, they made it to a stand of trees. On the back side of the trunks, grew a patch of flowers that matched the description that Aylan had given him. In short order, the blooms were in Thorn's basket, the imps were once again in hiding, and the thunder of the horses' galloping hooves rumbled across the ground as they carried the men across the stretch between the forest and the curtain wall.

Chapter 34
O Closeout O

Lazelan shivered as he replaced his footwear. Walking through the frigid pool was not something that he wanted to repeat any time soon. He missed the warmer climates of Ethik where he lived with his wife, Magdolyn. Just thinking of her warmed him to the core. Of course, the cloak helped too. He had given one to Aylan with the same magical properties. It would act as a shield from attacks either from metal or magic, as long as he wore it. But it functioned much like anything else; if there was a hole or some way for the magic to pass through, it would leave him vulnerable just like the way the rain always finds a way through a leaky roof.

He followed the wet footprints to the place where the dwarf was standing and looking up at the door. The mage began puzzling over the dwarven runes carved into the stone that barred their way, when Wolfbane caught up to them.

Lazelan had never been good at learning this language in school, and he could only make out the meaning of every second or third word. He knew enough though to recognize that it was some sort of spell. The dwarf looked up at him, pointed at the runes, and placed his hand over his throat. Lazelan turned to Wolfbane and placed a shushing finger in front of his lips. Then he simply let go of the energy being used to continue the bubble of silence. The tendril of energy snaked back toward his core, and he was glad to let it go. If they were going to meet this Carrier of the light, he was going to need all the energy he could muster.

As soon as the spell dropped, the ominous sound of the water dripping into the pool once again echoed through the cave. Odal read the passage that decorated the stone and the rock began to slide with the loud rumbling grating sound of stone on sand and rock. Lazelan had heard a similar racket in a water mill that had been used to grind grain, but the clamour in the cave was ten-fold. *There goes our element of surprise*, he thought wistfully.

The large slab moved at a snail's pace, but eventually, it left enough room for those inside to step out. Lazelan recognized the first one that approached as the blonde dwarf that had taken them to his rooms. Nalvo, his name was. The second dwarf to step through was shorter and fat, and had soft rabbit fur of a deep green decorating the cuffs and trim of his black leather ankle-length coat.

"That is Dain," Lazelan heard Odal say in low tones beside him. "He is the leader of the emerald clan, and the mage I was telling you about before."

Although Odal had professed earlier that he had only ever seen the dwarf being able to use the one spell, Lazelan knew better. In order to effect an area even as big as a tunnel, the dwarf mage would have had to have had years at his craft to work up to that scale with a variety of spells. Given Odal's reaction to Lazelan's scrying spell, he guessed that Dain had spent a good amount of time practicing his magic away from prying eyes. Now he only wondered if the man could still channel, or if he had been burned out long ago.

The third man to step through the opening was had a shaved head that stood at least a foot and a half taller than the dwarves he was with. The golden chain bearing the torch insignia that hung around his neck glinted as it caught the fire's glow from both sides. He had stepped through empty handed, but Lazelan wasn't fooled by his seemingly meek demeanor. Looking through the opening behind them, he could see a large tome on the table behind them that looked very much like the Almatraek Dim. It had to be its sister book, the book, the Almatraek Bright, at last.

"Odal, what brings you down here?" Nalvo asked in a mockingly congenial voice.

"They are here at the request of the king and queen, in search of a book of magic. In fact, that looks like it behind you, right there." Odal replied as if making a bland statement about the weather.

The Carriers face changed instantly. His eyes grew sharp, looking Lazelan's party up and down, trying to gauge their ability, and what trouble they might cause him. He seemed to be trying to affect a semblance of a smile, although it looked more like he was trying to keep his clamped together molars from gnashing. A soft red glow surrounded him, but Lazelan kept his ground, making sure that his cloak lay closed in front of him.

"Now, now," Dain intoned, "There is no need of that." When the glow still surrounded the Carrier a few moments later, the dwarf insisted. "Maewyn, please!" The red glow blinked out, and satisfied, Dain continued, apparently acting as mediator. "I'm sure that we can work this out."

"There is nothing to work out," Maewyn snapped. "The Carriers of Brightness have guarded the book for generations. It is being moved so that knaves such as these can't spirit it away."

"We need to search through its pages to see if there is a spell that can help the queen." Lazelan beseeched him. They needed to actually take the book, but for now, it was perhaps best to convince him that their cause wasn't evil by taking baby steps.

Maewyn seemed taken aback at the suggestion. "The book is not for ladies that wish to have more riches or perfect hair. She likely wouldn't be able to make heads nor tails of it anyway." Maewyn sneered.

Lazelan was affronted by the way this zealot was talking about his ruler. "Queen Aylan wishes for neither of those things." Lazelan answered indignantly, "She is a mage of notable ability, and she is very pregnant. The baby has somehow tapped into her powers, and is harming those around her. Surely, there must be a spell that can cloak the baby without shielding her or harming it. She is a good and noble queen who uses her magic to help her people. It would be detrimental to the kingdom to take her ability away from her."

"Surely the whole reason that a good book of magic exists is to help people." Dain reasoned. "Even if no one can possess the book, I'd wager that there is nothing in your prophecy that prohibits people from reading it."

Nalvo was very well versed in all of the teachings of the prophecy. He looked up to the Carrier as he confirmed the sentiment. "No, there is not."

Dain breathed an audible sigh of relief. "Well then, that's settled."

"Fools!" the Carrier boomed at the dwarves, "No one merely wants to read the book, these two have been ordered to return with it." Then to Lazelan and Wolfbane, he challenged, "Deny it if you dare."

"It is true, that we have been on a quest to retrieve it for the king and queen, but-"

"Ah-ha!" bellowed the Carrier as he seemed to grow another foot taller and wider.

Dain turned to walk back into the vault. "That shouldn't stop them from aiding the queen with her problem. How about I see what *I* can find."

"Stop!" yelled the Carrier, flinging his hand out toward Dain. An invisible blast to hit the dwarf and threw him across the room to collide with the wall. Dain fell to the ground and slumped there, unconscious. A chill ran up Lazelan's spine. The man was insane. He had just attacked an innocent person.

"Now, see here!" Nalvo protested, "You can't *do* that! We are clan chiefs, and we will decide what happens to the book while it is still in our possession. Perhaps it should remain guarded within these walls until *he who brightens the way*, himself, walks the land!"

Nalvo had planted himself between Maewyn and the Almatraek Bright, and he stood with his meaty fists on both hips. He looked as solid and as unmoveable as the rock around him. That is until he too was flung aside with a motion from the Carrier akin to shooing away a pestering fly. Lazelan's eyes followed the dwarf's course as Nalvo crashed into the stone shelf. A painfully sharp *crack* broke the temporary silence as he hit, then he too, lay crumpled and unmoving on the floor. Like with Dain, Lazelan could see the rise and fall of the dwarves' chests. They both still lived, at least for now, but there was no way of telling how severe their injuries were.

Anger and a feeling of helplessness had boiled up in Lazelan since the first attack, and now he was brimming with it. This is precisely what Lazelan had feared. This horrible display of Maewyn's feeling of entitlement proved that there was nothing that the peaceful dwarves could have said that would have convinced the Carrier of Brightness. He could not be reasoned with. Sadly, belief set in stone mixed with power did this to too many people. He was truly dangerous, and had already hurt the two unarmed dwarves. There was no holding back now. Beyond the book, this man had to be stopped.

Maewyn turned and took a step toward the vault as Odal freed the battle axe from its harness on his back. The dwarf hefted it with a practiced flourish that surprised Lazelan. Wolfbane drew his dagger and without hesitating, threw it at the Carrier's back. The long knife turned end over end through the air as it headed toward its mark. But just before it reached him, the dagger glanced off of something invisible without even stirring his clothing.

Lazelan used the second of a distraction to focus on the Almatraek Bright itself and cast a spell. "Flikt ot Ey," *Fly to me.* Nothing happened. He poured more energy into what was usually a simple spell. The book quivered on the table top, the cover making a low drumming sound against the wood.

"What?" Maewyn asked in amazement, and turned to the party that still stood. "Magic isn't supposed to be able to touch the book. How are you doing that? What form of darkness is this?" he hissed.

Lazelan didn't justify the question with a remark. He only poured more energy into the spell. What had started as a tendril of power was now as thick as a tree trunk. He wasn't going to be able to cast for much longer. His pool of energy was almost used up from the spells cast throughout the day. He hadn't had time to rest, but he wasn't going to give up. The book slid an inch toward him on the table.

"Impossible!" Maewyn cried, and created an entrapment spell to surround Lazelan.

As soon as Lazelan heard the incantation for what the Carrier was trying to cast, he dropped his own spell and lowered his arm to let his cloak fall shut. Behind the Carrier, the book ceased its shuttering and lay like it had lain on the table forever.

Maewyn's bonds of magic hit Lazelan right as the material drew together. The spell dissipated with a green glowing puff of smoke upon settling on his protective cloak. Maewyn seemed to be swallowed in frustration. He bared his teeth and turned to run the few feet to the table. He scooped up the book and hugged the heavy leather-bound tome to his chest.

Lazelan did the only thing that he could think of. He threw up a shield across the doorway of the vault so that the Carrier of Brightness couldn't come back out. Maewyn didn't seem to understand what had been done at first, until he attempted to saunter out of the cramped room. He hit the barrier with his toe, in the middle of what should have been a full stride. He squinted at the other mage and threw his shoulder against the blockage, evidently trying to get through.

At the added pressure of the Carrier's impact, Lazelan's spell was strained, causing him to use more energy to maintain it. He could feel his energy waning. "The door!" Lazelan directed Odal, who stood with his axe, at the ready to advance. The dwarf called out the memorized words that would seal the vault, and the door began to slide shut at its infuriatingly slow pace.

Now the Carrier took a few steps back before he launched himself at the closing doorway. The momentum mixed with the combined weight of Maewyn and the book almost broke Lazelan's spell. The shield seemed to bend outward for a split second before bouncing back into place like a string on a lute. The only sound that was produced though was a low grunt from Lazelan as he gritted his teeth and a bead of sweat trickled down the side of his forehead despite the cold of the cavern around him.

The stone door had slid halfway across by now, but a snail could have outpaced it. A smile of triumph flashed across Maewyn's face. This time, he took a few more steps further back before charging.

Lazelan knew that he wasn't going to be able to handle the pressure this time. He quickly re-adjusted the spell to only cover what was left of the opening. Maewyn was going to have to saddle through sideways if he was going to make it, which meant that Lazelan could pour more strength into that part of the shield where the other mage's shoulder would try to penetrate.

Odal ran to stand beside the doorway, and held his axe aloft, ready to bring it down the second that the mage burst through. Lazelan began to sway where he stood, and Wolfbane tried to steady him. Maewyn leaned forward as if to charge, but instead of moving, he hurled a bolt of lightning at what was left of the shield. The electric flash shattered the already weakened spell in a place that Lazelan hadn't been ready for. He fell as it passed through easily like a hot knife through butter, and the temperature rose with its heat.

Odal's axe came down at the sign of movement, and sparks fanned upward as the honed blade struck nothing but stone floor with a harsh *clank*. The lightning bolt struck the wall behind Wolfbane, and Lazelan could feel every hair on his body trying to stand on end.

Maewyn tried to come through the thin opening, but Odal's body was barring his way. Before the Carrier could act, and at the risk of the dwarf getting a limb crushed in the closing space between the stone door and the wall, he forcefully pushed the mage back inside with his bare hand.

Odal pulled his arm free in the nick of time as the door closed the gap, came to a standstill, and the grinding of the moving stone stopped.

No one spoke. Only the ever dripping water back down the hall, and the picks overhead made any sound. Odal examined his axe blade, and Lazelan, who could only kneel there, placed a hand on Wolfbane's shoulder in thanks for his help.

That's when the first earth rattling boom came from inside the vault. Lazelan could hear Odal's breath catch as the two torches on the wall shook in their sconces. They looked around at the tunnel around them, searching for any sign of what was happening. Lazelan felt the ground shake for a moment as the sound erupted again.

"I think he's trying to force his way out." Wolfbane hedged nervously.

"It won't work," Odal told them. As he spoke, his words became more paranoid. "It's enchanted to be unmoveable except when the words are spoken by a clan chief. He'll bring the cave down around us before the thing moves."

Almost as if it had been ominously summoned, the next booming blast hit. Small shards of rock rained down onto the terrified party, and one of the sconces came loose from the wall, spilling the torch to the ground where it was snuffed out. Hairline fractures in the rock walls and ceiling became visible with a symphony of sharp popping cracking noises. The water that had been intermittently dripping into the pool, now came out in a steady trickle. Perhaps most ominously, the methodical picking of axes from the tunnels above halted entirely.

"We have to stop him," Lazelan warned, "Odal, perhaps you should open the door again. We can deal with those consequences when they happen. It's better than him killing us all!"

Odal began to say the words once again that would cause the giant stone to begin its sideways trek. However, with only five words left, the final boom hit and the rock above came down on top of them.

Chapter 35
O Bouquet O

Oslan's party pelted through the postern gates with clods of packed dirt flying from their horses' hooves. They passed the market, and raced back into the courtyard of the castle. Several servants jumped out of the way of the oncoming stallions so as not to be trampled. Oslan hardly noticed them as he focussed on getting to the doors of the keep.

As they rounded the corner, Oslan saw Stanton Sprig's squire and a servant, likely the seer's handmaid, in an animated discussion together on the steps of the keep.

"Cal!" Oslan called as he reined in his mount. The boy came running over immediately.

"Yes, Your Majesty?" he asked with a bow.

"There's no time for that," Oslan said roughly, "Where is the queen?"

"She's in the throne room, Sire, meeting with Augden Zalice."

The king didn't miss a beat. He leapt from his horse, and taking the basket from Thorn, started to bound up the steps of the keep. He made it to the top step before loose mud on his boot caused him to slip. He went sprawling face first through the doors being held open by the palace guards. Flowers, roots, stems, and leaves went in every direction as the basket tumbled across the floor.

Face reddened with embarrassment, Oslan didn't bother to stop to brush himself off. So desperate to get to his queen was he that he could have had a broken bone and not known it. He would see to himself later. He left the basket, collecting all the items off the floor into a crude bouquet, and ran with it to meet his wife.

What's she doing with that scoundrel? Oslan fumed. He understood the effects of what he was about to hand her, and it made him angry to realize that she was probably going to need the herbologist's help. But this was the man that had hypnotized Cal, and had forced him to steal the signet rings of many nobles in Endalwynndale. Augden's lust for power had gotten too big for the man. Sure, he had turned around and had helped after a fashion when they had needed his aid, but still, Oslan didn't trust him as far as an imp could throw him.

The guards that stood sentinel outside the throne room saw him coming and pulled open the double doors before he got there. He strode across the floor, still half at a run even though it wasn't a very regal way of making an entrance. That mattered little right now.

Aylan sat on her gilded throne, in a dark green gown. She wore a delicate golden royal circlet. It bore a bloom of dragon's breath, the kingdom's national flower, and dangling below, a gold-slashed tigers-eye gemstone decorated her smooth brow. She often favoured this instead of her heavier queen's crown. Even with the dark half-moons under her eyes and the weariness that etched her face, he thought that she was beautiful. Augden Zalice was standing at the foot of the stairs, speaking with her.

Without so much as a pardon, Oslan brushed passed the man, out of breath, but relieved that he had made it in time. He handed the bouquet to Aylan, not realizing that she was recoiling from the plants. She took them gingerly, and her brow furrowed as she held and examined them.

"Something isn't right," observed Augden from his place on the floor.

"Of course it is, we got everything on the list." Oslan replied, perhaps a little too petulantly.

"Everything appears to be in order," Aylan started, "but nothing's happening."

"Well, maybe it takes longer to work when the plants are fresh?" the king hedged. Both the queen and Augden shook their heads.

"Fresh herbs are more potent, if anything." Augden corrected him.

"Do you remember when Zaltreous was held prisoner here and he hid the packets in Carn's armour?" she explained, "As soon as he came near me-"

Her words were cut off by the sound of a scuffle in the hallway.

"You must let me *in!*" came an urgent voice muffled by the heavy oak doors.

"Who is there?" Oslan demanded.

The door swung outward, admitting Cal, who raced up the throne room with what appeared to be the empty basket that the king had left behind. He was too out of breath to speak as he called up the room to the queen. "I think the king meant for you to have this!" She rose and started forward toward the top of the steps to meet him as he closed the distance between them. He raced up the steps without waiting for permission and handed the basket to the queen, who instantly fell in a swoon.

Two guards raced to catch her, but Oslan wasn't about to let her fall. He caught her easily and sat her back on the throne, supporting her as the guards cleared the throne room of any that weren't involved.

"Cal finally caught his breath and said, "Is she alright, Sire? I only brought the basket because there was something still left inside. It was only a couple of stems with small yellow flowers, but I figured that they might be important.

"Now, we're in business!" cried Augden excitedly as he rubbed his hands together as if to warm them. "Boy, go get me some pieces of cloth, it's time that I get to making some packets."

*   *   *

Light flickered to life, interrupting Sasha's dreamless slumber. A succession of pictures and brief scenes flooded her mind. She saw people; short, stout people with long hair and beards, all falling. They were carrying weapons or tools, she didn't exactly know which. Then she saw Wolfbane. He was smiling. Smiling at her? Her vision stayed for a while as she admired the lines of his face and his dark grey eyes that were so like a cloud before a winter storm. There was so much warmth in those eyes when he smiled. Then Lazelan swam into view. He was facing a stone wall. He was weak. He had no way out. Then a dwarf held a book, a big book with straps that buckled around it. The vision changed again, and she saw a bald man. He was wearing the golden pendant that had haunted her visions for days. He seemed to be denying something, and shaking his head in negation. Then the same man was tugging on Wolfbane's sleeve. Something streaked through the air toward them. It was red and as fast as an arrow.

A groan interrupted her vision, making her begin the ascent through the levels of her subconscious mind, to return her to the waking world.

I'm alive! she marvelled. She felt a rough woolen blanket under her fingertips. A soft pillow lay under her head as she rolled her head toward the sound that had woken her. She was in a bed in the hospice. Beside her, Millie groaned again. Sasha felt like a great weight had been lifted from her. Her visions were once again free from darkness, and there was no pull on her from any spells that she could sense. The instant feeling of relief and elation that washed over her was rudely interrupted though by the realization that she was indeed free. That left her with only questions; *What has happened to the queen? How has Lazelan been trapped?* and *Will they ever make it home?*

Chapter 36
O Tunnel Vision O

Screams and shouts of alarm filled the air as rock, rubble, and dwarves tumbled down from above. Chunks of stone splashed into the water until it piled high enough that the only sound left was rock hitting rock. Lazelan used the last ounce of his energy to form a wall of protection above them, but it didn't last long. As the weight of the stone tried to flatten them, each slab and boulder that impacted the shield weakened his spell until the pressure finally gave way.

Moans of pain from strange voices, and hacking coughs caused by everyone trying to breathe the settling dust broke the momentary silence after the cave-in. They were trapped in pitch black, the one remaining torch having been extinguished by a falling rock, or perhaps by the plume of dust that arose from the falling debris.

The particles floating around that entered his lungs with every breath made it seem like Lazelan was trying to breathe through a soaked cloth, with barely any life-saving air getting through. He coughed, trying to clear the buildup in his lungs. The mage felt the pressure of something on his leg, and pushed at it with his hand. A smoothed wooden pick-axe handle with the added weight of a slab of rock leaned on his limb, and he was thankful that it hadn't been the other end of the pick that had hit him on the way down.

He tried to get his bearings, but found it almost impossible in the confusion of what had happened, and with no light. He would have cast a fireball if he could have, but he didn't think at this point, that he would even have been able to light a candle if he had to rely on magic to do it.

One after another, voices started to call out to one another.

"Bazgin, where are you?" A deep voice called from somewhere across the cave.

"O're here!" another base voice answered back from a spot closer to the mage.

"Dolin, did ye make it, lad?" A concerned gravelly voice demanded.

"Aye, Papa, I'm well." a much younger voice replied.

"Baern!" Shouted a desperate female voice from somewhere nearby. "Baern! By the shields of the army of Ormond, man, say something if you're alive!"

"I'm here, Tarla, fear not," a pained, yet fond voice answered, "You'll not be rid of me that easily, lass."

"Gildir, are you there?" the voice of an older dwarf sung out. To this inquiry, there was no answer.

"Nalvo, Dain?" Lazelan recognized that one as belonging to Odal. *Good, at least he survived.* Lazelan thought. Then he called out to his other friend.

"Wolfbane, are you alright?" the mage asked shakily. His little friend groaned beside him directly to his left. The sounds of a shifting body, a small avalanche of pebbles and sliding sand, and the gnome's leather armour creaking told Lazelan that he was presumably trying to sit up or stand.

"What happened?" Wolfbane asked. It was Odal that started to answer. "The Carrier of Brightness caused the tunnel to collapse. The miners above us fell through when their floor gave out."

From the other side of the cavern, Maewyn shouted a command in a crazed growl, "Give it to me this instant or I'll take it from you myself!"

"Ah!" came Nalvo's jittery squeal. A red spark in the darkness momentarily flashed above the Carrier's fingertips and winked out. Several of the miners gasped.

"Drat!" the Carrier screamed. "Still, that doesn't mean that I still can't take it from you with my bare hands!"

"What is the meaning of this?" yelled one of the dwarves. "We are likely going to die down here, and you two are fighting like a couple of ninnies!"

"He's right," Odal concurred. "Our first priority should be a light source. Without a torch or a lantern or something, we'll never find our way out of this mess. I can feel a draft from above us, so likely that means that the way up there is still clear. But it's not good enough to find a way to climb out of this hole; if we can't see, we won't be able to read the runes to find our way back to our clans."

Lazelan was beginning to understand why this man had become the chief of the tigers-eyes. He had a talent for keeping his head and finding priorities in an emergency situation.

"I can perhaps help with that," Wolfbane offered. Lazelan heard the gnome's boots scuffing the sand on the floor as he stood. The gnome whispered a quiet oath, or perhaps it was a prayer. "If there's any brightness left in the world, please let it still work, we could use some of it here."

Then about two feet off the ground, a hair's breadth of silver light stung Lazelan's eyes, and a blinding fire pierced the darkness as Wolfbane drew the rest of his fiery scimitar from its sheath.

Every being in the cavern gasped as flames that seemed almost as bright as the sun licked out from the blade of the magic weapon. As the gnome held it aloft, the brilliant light lit up every corner of the cavern, and the faces of those within it. Although there were many evident injuries, it appeared that miraculously, everyone had survived. Dwarves began to get to their feet, some moving rocks off of their trapped comrades, and others using fallen tools as levers to raise slabs too heavy to simply lift.

The stone door was the only undamaged artifact, standing proudly and still where they had left it. Around it, lay ruins. Beyond the door, Nalvo stood with his back up against a wall of rubble, clutching the tome as if he were a drowning victim and it was keeping him afloat. He started to sidle sideways as for the moment, he seemed to have been forgotten.

The Carrier had turned his back to the dwarf and now stood with his mouth hanging open at the sight of Wolfbane's sword. The gnome walked the perimeter of the space that the cave-in had left them with. The tunnel they had come down was completely blocked off. Behind the door, the vault had been almost completely destroyed. Scorch marks marred the walls where some of the shelves had stood, presumably from whatever spell the Carrier had been trying to use to escape. Sadly, piles of ash that had been unreplaceable scrolls and books at one time, now lay littered all over the place. Dain seemed to have sustained no further injury, but he still lay unconscious, so they couldn't know yet for sure.

Then the gnome looked upward. There was a jagged hole in what used to be the ceiling that ran above a good section of what was left of their tunnel. A nice pile of rubble led up to it at one end.

"Have no fear, follow me. We seem to have an easy way out! Let's get everyone out of here." The gnome told Odal, and started to pick his way up the hill of boulders.

"Alright, everyone, there seems to be a spot where we can climb out." The chief of the tigers-eye clan began to give orders. "Stay together now. Baern, Tarla, do you think that you can manage to bring Dain out of this?" The dwarven couple nodded their heads and set out to lift him from the wreckage, each one supporting him by ducking under one of his arms and dragging him along. "Nalvo, you walk with me, and don't let that book out of your hands. Whatever the rest of you do, keep an eye on that Carrier of Brightness. He is not to be trusted." A few faces still looked dazed from their experience, but they nodded and placed themselves around Maewyn like an escort. The Carrier didn't object, and allowed himself to be led by the group.

They climbed up the hill of fallen rock, some limping, other's gingerly supporting an arm, or walking with a torn bit of shirt against a cut here or there. Lazelan had no idea how long the dancing flames would continue to burn, but he wasn't worried about it petering out. Most enchanted items never lost their power.

Wolfbane led the way and held his sword high for Odal to carefully check each set of runes. As they passed into more familiar territory, they began to hear excited voices up ahead. As the light from the gnome's flaming sword mingled with the torchlight of a group of miners that had run from the sounds of the cracking rock, a mighty cheer welled up from the crowd of workers that were waiting for an all-clear to be able to go back down the shaft to rescue their friends. The two groups met as hearty hugs, pats on the back, and even tears of happiness touched almost everyone. The Carrier however, was staring at Wolfbane as if he had seen a ghost.

●

Chapter 37
O Fight or Flight O

Aylan sat at the table in the chair to Oslan's right, rather uncomfortably. Augden had been busy making packets all afternoon to find the right balance of herbs for someone of Aylan's size. It stood to reason that the batch that had come from Zaltreous' cell had prevented him from casting, but hadn't weakened him to a state of unconsciousness as they had with Aylan. Therefore, it must just be a matter of finding the right amount of each plant to stunt her magic use, but leave her conscious and able to do her job as queen.

It had taken several hours of making and breaking packets until a mixture that was suitable had been found. The queen had fainted dead away more often than not during these trials, and the result of a particularly weak package of herbs had left Augden trying to wrestle the thing out of the air. After that, they had kept at least one in the room at all times until the next one was ready to be tested. In the end, the middle-aged man had succeeded.

It left Aylan with a woozy feeling that she wasn't a fan of. This would do in a pinch, but there had to be a better solution. She could sense that her pool of energy was still there. But with a pouch of material full of herbs hanging on a leather thong around her neck, it was almost as if her abilities were dulled so that she couldn't reach out to dip into it. Fortunately, the baby also seemed unable to access her reserves. Her vigour had remained at the same level, but every once in a while she could feel a disturbance in her core, followed by a sharp kick from the child. *I feel like that sometimes when I'm frustrated too*, she thought regretfully.

Oslan's family was gathered around the table to sup together, which she thought would be a wonderful distraction. As it turned out though, the packet was proving to make the meal quite a frustrating endeavour.

She reached for her goblet and missed. Double vision had accompanied headaches brought on by the prolonged exposure to the temporary cure. Augden had offered to try adjusting the herbs again, but she had told him not to bother. She was exhausted, and was patiently waiting for Lazelan to bring her news of the book. At least these were good enough for now to allow her to take a nap without worrying that she was going to burn the castle to the ground.

She tried reaching for her cup again and her fingers drew up short of the stem. Oslan took pity on her. He rose slightly to reach from his place at the head of the table, picked up the glass and handed it to her. His face was full of concern. She thanked him and took a sip of the refreshing spiced wine.

When her mind was on other things, it was generally easy to go through the motions of a meal. But it was hard to keep up appearances just now when she couldn't even pick up a cup without aid.

She was trying to follow the conversation at the table, but she was worried about Millie and Sasha, who were reported to still be unconscious in the hospice the last time she had been informed. She knew that she had taken too much. She wished that she had been able to stop the spell sooner, but there was no way that she could have made sure that they would be ok if she passed out alongside them.

She knew that once they had gotten a good sleep, they would be fine, but the waiting to make sure was just so hard. In the end, she hadn't given the guards any explanation at all; she had just given them an order. They hadn't questioned her, they had just gotten help. Sometimes there were advantages of being a queen.

She tried to stab a piece of fish with her fork and missed. She saw Oslan immediately reach a hand toward her, and she shook her head to ward him off. Thankfully he noticed and backed off, however, the motion of shaking her head made it reel once more. She tried to massage her forehead with her fingertips to make it stop.

"Can I get anything for you, dear?" the queen mother asked very sweetly from her spot across from Aylan. It brought her attention back to the meal. Surprisingly, the woman who had seemed so vehemently opposed to their marriage in the first place, had become a good ally to the Aylan since she had quickened.

"No, thank you," Aylan smiled warmly back. "Really, I'm fine, and this won't be forever. Lazelan will get back soon, I'm sure." *He has to.*

*　　　*　　　*

All six clan chiefs had been called to a meeting. They sat in a close room at a large rectangular table with Lazelan and Wolfbane, who also occupied two chairs. One seat remained empty, as Maewyn had refused to sit. No one was worried, though. Although old habits seemed to have died hard with the mage, he appeared to have been cowed. His magic, along with Lazelan's, had been tapped. Not forever, but at least until they had each had a chance to have a couple of hearty meals and catch a good night's sleep for their pools of energy to replenish themselves.

The thick table in front of them was laden with an array of steaming hot foods. Heavy metal wine goblets encrusted with jewels sat in front of each man or dwarf, and two giant candelarba shed light on the gathering.

Lazelan was surprised to see that this cave's walls held no trace of any of the clan's gems that were prevalent throughout the mountain. Although polished smooth, the walls were a uniform dark brown-grey colour that was only marred by darker or lighter lines that represented different age-old layers of the rock. Odal had explained that this room had been chosen on purpose as a meeting place for the clan chiefs, so that the bland space would create a sense of neutrality between the leaders. All of their big decisions were made here.

Lazelan raised a piece of meat to his lips and took a hearty bite. The warmth was soothing, and the morsel tasted absolutely scrumptious. This would have been a feast if not for the serious topic at hand. No one spoke. The clan chiefs were split down the middle on where the book should go.

"Enough of this *stony* silence," Wolfbane begged, "Can we have the book or not?"

"The very fact that the queen, *our* queen has requested it is reason enough for me to hand it over." Dain said. "After what has happened here today, I wouldn't be unhappy to see it go."

"But we were charged with the task of guarding it generations ago." Agamm argued. "We were never supposed to relinquish it until a Carrier came to retrieve it, and now one has. Is our blood oath worth so little? The existence of this book spans way beyond the life of one queen."

"This tome was made to help protect people." Odal put forth. "The queen needs its aid now. What is the point of even making a book of protection spells, if it can't be used for good when it is truly needed?"

"But who is to decide when it is required?" Durlak asked in his creaky aged voice. "That was the point of our oath. Before they were wiped out, the last member of the Council of Mages gave the book to a Carrier and it was decided that the Carriers of Brightness alone should make that decision."

"You are all missing the point." Nalvo interjected. He had been strangely silent this whole time, not like his usual blustery self. "The Carriers were charged with keeping the book safe until *he who brightens the way* walks upon the land." He looked to Maewyn pointedly as he said it, and although he hadn't been seeking confirmation, the bald man regretfully nodded his agreement. "The Carriers get to decide where it stays until then. That was the oath we agreed to."

"Exactly," Azagut agreed. "Then it is plain that Maewyn here should take the book with him."

"No," Nalvo disagreed. "I'm not sure that I'd hand the book over to Carrier Azemar even if it was the right thing to do. He has directly endangered too many dwarves when the Carriers are supposed to stand for all that is bright in the world. But no matter the severity of his wrongdoing, the final resting place of the book sits among us."

"Well said, my boy," Durlak congratulated him. "Should we wait for another Carrier then, or are we to watch over it forever? I mean, none of us really believes that *he who brightens the way* will ever really come." Then he shot an apologetic look at Nalvo. "Well," he added a tad sheepishly, "Except maybe for you. But I agree that it is clear that this Carrier is crooked."

"Wait, then we keep it?" demanded Agamm, confused.

"No." Nalvo responded calmly. *"He who brightens the way* has already come. In fact, he eats at our table now."

Durlak nearly choked on the bite that he was chewing. Four of the dwarves erupted in argument all at once. Nalvo and Odal exchanged a glance, the only two that sat silent.

Then Nalvo pushed aside his plate and unrolled a wooden scroll from his personal library. It was a copy of the prophecy. The Carrier standing in the corner began to look ill. Nalvo motioned for silence and then began to read aloud from the parchment.

"Ye shall recognize the chosen one only in the face of a miracle in a time of darkness. He shall bring light to the blackness, like a beacon in the night. He shall gather non-believers and believers alike as followers, and shall lead them from the dark into a world of brightness. Forever after, he shall be known as *He who Brightens the Way.*"

Lazelan forgot to chew. He hadn't made the connection before, but now it seemed as plain as day. "Wolfbane, you gathered together and led almost fifty dwarves to safety today by the light of your sword. Most of them think the prophecy holds no credence, but Nalvo was among us, and he does. You brought the brightness to the dark, and I don't think that anyone that was there would disagree that the flame that it produces was like a beacon in the darkness of the cave."

All heads swivelled to the gnome. Maewyn licked his lips in nervousness. It was obvious that things had been taken well out of his hands. He would have no power over the book now. Wolfbane dropped the chicken leg he had been eating, and held up his hands in protest as if he could fend off their stares. Reading the word that had been branded into the gnome's palm, Maewyn Azemar instantly fell to his knees, prostrating himself.

"What just happened? Agamm asked, still completely muddled. In response, Nalvo continued to read.

"The Chosen One shall be marked as such, so that even the non-believers might be enlightened."

"Jarusiyat." the mage breathed. "The Amatraek Bright belongs to you."

●

Chapter 38
O Fight or Flight O

The food had strengthened Lazelan, however, without having slept, he was still too weak to cast even the most meagre spell. He had finally been allowed to look through the pages of the Almatraek Bright to find a spell that would solve the queen's problem and keep those around her safe. With so many treasures held within the pages, Lazelan found it hard to stay on track. But finally, about a third of the way through, he located something useful.

"I have it!" he cried excitedly. Wolfbane travelled the short distance across the space behind the red doors. They had been waiting for their eyes to adjust to the the sun outside that now seemed so harsh. Every time the light became comfortable, the guards would open one door by a fraction more. It was almost time to go now, and Lazelan couldn't have been happier.

"This spell can be used to enchant a shawl or a blanket that the queen can wrap around her belly. It will confuse the babe if it tries to reach into her pool, preventing it from being able to find her energy source at all. As long as the queen keeps the garment off of her own head, her mind won't be affected at all. Lazelan marked the page and snapped the heavy tome shut, taking the time to re-buckle both of the leather straps that held it safely closed.

Odal and Nalvo had come to see them off, and a group of dwarves with an array of weapons were present to make sure that the Carrier also left without a fight. There had been talk at the meeting of the clan chiefs as to whether Maewyn should be kept in the dungeons as punishment for the destruction and mayhem he had caused. However, none of the dwarves wanted to have to worry about him, nor the probable threat of a rescue attempt that might be made by the other Carriers of Brightness should he fail to come home. The dwarves really just wanted him gone so that life could resume its regular monotony.

Maewyn, for his part, had been reluctant to go, especially since it would be his job to return to the compound where the Carriers of Brightness lived, and share the story of what had happened here. He would have to explain why he had arrived without the book.

Lazelan imagined that Maewyn would be feeling quite lost; now that the chosen one had surfaced, what were all of the Carriers to do? Their purpose had been to protect the book and to spread the word of the prophecy so that all would recognize *he who brightens the way*, when he came. Now it seemed that they would have no purpose.

Maewyn must have been thinking the same thing, as he strode over to Wolfbane wearing an expression on his face as if he had just gotten the best idea in the world. This was the first amount of liveliness that had shone in Maewyn's eyes since he had lost possession of the Almatraek Bright. That was worrisome.

"You should come with me to the compound, then the others can meet you and we can learn from your ways!" the Carrier entreated the gnome.

"I can't," Wolfbane answered simply, "I must get back to Endalwynndale with the big book of magic to save the queen."

Like a wild animal turning to bite the hand that feeds it, anger suddenly flashed in the Carrier's eyes at the refusal of his new plan. He grabbed the gnome's arm, perhaps a little too roughly.

Wolfbane smiled calmly up at Maewyn, and called out the single word: "Guards!"

In less than a heartbeat, Lazelan heard a forceful exhalation of breath, and a streak of red shot through the air, finding its mark in the side of Maewyn's neck. The dart's red flights stuck out quite visibly against the mage's coppery skin, as the thing quivered in his jugular with the next two pulses of his heart. The light poison on the tip of it worked quickly, and the Carrier dropped like a stone, unconscious.

"He will sleep for the next few hours," the guard assured them. "It should give you a well-earned head start. Now, my friends, I think that it is time for you to leave us."

The dwarves made their goodbyes, and Nalvo even went so far as to hug the gnome before he left with a tear in his eyes. "I always believed in you," the dwarf told the gnome before he let go.

"My mother always told me the same thing." Wolfbane replied.

"I'm sure that your mother was an amazing woman," Nalvo told him, then added excitedly: "but I bet she didn't have a griffin!"

Soon enough, Lazelan and Wolfbane had been properly introduced to Nalvo's precious mount. It didn't take long before they were perched on the animal's back, and the griffin jumped into the air with a screech and an unsettling lurch. The two adventurers turned to wave farewell, and then they were smoothly soaring off toward the east and Endalwynndale, mistakenly thinking that now they might get the book back to the castle scot-free.

~ The End of Book Four ~

●

Dear Adventurer,

Thank you for joining our heroes during their trials and victory in the bowels of Mount Embalk, and for believing against hope in something bright. You learned that a game of strategy and chance can be manipulated, and that even someone that's a cheat can be made to see the light. You witnessed the selflessness of friendship, and that even a mighty king might stoop to serve the one he loves.

As Lazelan and Wolfbane attempt to return to the castle, something stands to get in their way. Will the pages of the Almatraek Dim finally be able to be erased, and if so, what repercussions might that bring with it? Our adventure will continue in book five, as Wolfbane takes a new party of knights to travel to the far reaches of Endalwynndale. Desperate to find answers about what in fact happened to the members of the lost Council of Mages, will they be able to help prevent Aylan, Oslan, and all of their royal subjects from suffering the same fate?

Till A Quest Calls Again,

Heather Reilly

Now you, too, can enjoy the game of

ᴋINGDOM

In this race to rule the kingdom, gem-carrying subjects will flock to you, but not all may join your clan. You must work quickly to usher the right subjects together before your opponents try to sabotage your rise to the throne. The thief, seer, and mage are only some of the characters your opponents can use to attempt to thwart your efforts. There are others to help you, but they can turn on you in a flash as sneaky manoeuvres are fair game, and there is no treason without a kingdom.

For more information, visit the author's website at

www.booksofafeather.weebly.com